The Ruination of Dan Becker

THE RUINATION
OF
DAN BECKER

ROBIN GIBSON

AVALON BOOKS
THOMAS BOUREGY AND COMPANY, INC.
401 LAFAYETTE STREET
NEW YORK, NEW YORK 10003

PRINTED IN THE UNITED STATES OF AMERICA
BY HADDON CRAFTSMEN, SCRANTON, PENNSYLVANIA

To the memory of my dad, Glen Gibson

Chapter One

I felt tired enough to drop from my saddle when I topped the ridge and spotted that little ole town. Even from a distance, I could tell it wasn't much, but I was glad to see it, and so was my horse. Me and that horse had come a long ways together. Though I wasn't hurrying, we'd made good time. The heat and the dust had been awful this last week, robbing both of us of our strength. That horse had been with me for quite a spell, and he knew that town meant rest in a cool stable, some hay, and, if he was lucky, some corn too.

Not much could be said for that town. It was only a row of buildings on either side of a dusty street. But my guess was that it would have a saloon and a livery, which were all I needed.

As I was just wandering around the country, I wasn't on any regular trail. I

1

was coming up on that town from behind, so I pointed that horse for the back of the general store.

About a hundred yards from the store, I saw something that didn't set right. Two women were sweating and loading supplies on a wagon while two men lounged lazily nearby. Sensing something wasn't right, I stopped and shucked my Winchester. Folks have laughed at me for being overly cautious, but some of them folks are dead now. It pays to be careful, especially in times like these, where many a man has been killed for his horse.

Suddenly, those two men stepped forward and said something to the women. Tipping my Winchester over my right shoulder, I touched a spur to that horse and we started down to the store. That horse didn't like things any better than I did, 'cause he walked slow and easy. That horse knew that when I slid out my rifle, we were coming up on trouble.

One of the men stepped in front of the women, blocking their path. While I couldn't hear what he said, I sure heard the angry reply:

"I wouldn't sell to Ketchum, not even if he was the last man on earth!"

The speaker was a short, pretty woman of about twenty. She had red hair and right now her face was about as red. Her green eyes were snapping fire at those two men. Her companion was also pretty, and from their features I judged them to be sisters. The younger one had blond hair, and that was the only thing I could see that kept them from being identical.

They were facing me, but if they saw me, they were paying me no mind. The two hired guns had their backs to me and seemed to be unaware of my presence. Oh, I recognized the breed all right. These two had the slow, insolent manner common to paid warriors.

"You best think it over, missy. There ain't no way you two can run a ranch by yourselves," the taller gun hand threatened.

As if to prove his point, he reached out and knocked a sack from the redhead's arms. The sack opened on the ground and beans spilled out.

Still some twenty yards away, I

stopped, and with a flick of my wrist I jacked a shell into the chamber of my Winchester. When those men heard me behind them, their backs stiffened. Tipping my rifle back against my shoulder, I enjoyed watching them squirm.

Smiling with genuine pleasure, I waited. I could almost read their minds. They dearly wanted to turn, but were afraid to move. The women turned their shocked gazes on me. The redhead looked at me with distrust while the blonde merely appeared curious.

"Looks like you got the drop on us, friend," the tall gunman said softly. He didn't seem to be overly worried, though.

I laughed and said, "Turn around and let me see what kind of coyote I caught."

Slowly, the gunmen turned, and I knew at once that the tall one was top dog. He had a thin, cruel-looking face, but what set him apart was his eyes. They held neither hate nor fear. They just looked dead.

The other one was shorter and broader, with a face that one could easily forget. His features were even and plain, and his fleshy face showed a look of surprise when he saw my rifle pointed skyward. Quickly he glanced at his partner. Right then I knew that he wouldn't start anything till his partner did.

That tall feller was contemplating makin' a play, and I was sure hoping he wouldn't. Those women were right in my line of fire, and if it came to a shooting match, chances were they might get hurt. Not that I was worried about missing, but a .44 can go right through a man.

"Go ahead. Try it if you feel lucky," I taunted them with a smile. "At this range you might miss with them short guns, but I won't with this rifle."

The tall man didn't move his head, but I got the impression that he nodded. Maybe it was the way his body relaxed, but I knew he would wait. He had used his gun before and felt no need to prove his courage right then. He had been in situations like this. I could feel it.

As if he were reading my mind, the other gunman said, "You wouldn't be talking that way if you knew who this was. That's Garland Chase, the fastest gun around!"

Garland Chase! I'd heard of him, and if what I'd heard was true, he was mighty good with that weapon he carried. Being a man who likes to play poker, I've never seen the sense in letting folks know what you're thinking, so I kept my face still when I heard the name, but it had given me quite a shock.

"Shut up, Wes," Chase said angrily. It was the first emotion he had shown. "I hope you'll be sticking around," he told me. "It'll save me the trouble of looking for you."

I looked at him and laughed even though I didn't much feel like it. "I'll be around."

Satisfied, he motioned to Wes and they left. Then I turned my attention to the ladies, who were staring at me like they thought I was crazy or something.

Maybe I was a wild-looking creature to them, 'cause me and my horse were both covered with about ten pounds of dust. My hair needed cutting and it had been a long time since I'd shaved.

"Ladies, you ought to know enough to

get the heck out of the way when men start talking gun talk," I scolded mildly.

"Of all the. . . . Just who do you think you are? What's your name?" the red-head cried, her face flaming to match her hair.

That got my dander up some. After all, I had just helped them out of a tight spot. Anyway, why should she care who I was? Although angered, I managed to keep my voice even as I answered. "Folks call me Becker. Now, you'd best let me help you load that wagon."

"Becker? Is that it?" the blonde asked in a friendly voice. Looking closer, I could see that her hair had a reddish tint to it.

"It gets me by," I said, getting down from my horse.

"I'm Kitty McCray, and this is my sister, Laura," the blonde said, smiling brightly.

"Pleased," I grunted, and picked up the torn sack of beans.

It took me most of an hour to load the wagon. Each time I went inside, I glared at the storekeeper, who cowered behind the counter. Why the heck wasn't he helping them load the wagon? Something was wrong here. Western men didn't treat women like that. And why were those two gun hands makin' trouble for them? In most places, bothering women that way would earn a week in jail.

My mind puzzled over it as I stacked the supplies on the wagon. I was tempted to ask Laura, but I had the feeling she would tell me it was none of my business, which I guess it wasn't. Still, I was curious.

I had to grin. Most times I would rather take a beating than load supplies. To make matters worse, they were buying enough supplies to feed an army.

"Thank you, Mr. Becker," Kitty said when I had finished. "Perhaps you'd like to ride out and join us for supper?"

Immediately, she got a look from her sister that would stop a stampede. Just to be ornery, I accepted. Besides, it was getting on into the afternoon and I was hungry.

So with that redhead glaring at me like she wished I was dead, I tied my horse to the back of the wagon and climbed aboard.

As we drove out to the ranch, I studied the countryside. It was good cow country, but not nearly as good as other land I had crossed this morning. Ketchum must want their place powerfully bad to be trying to frighten them off.

Another thing bothered me: What in the world were two women doing running a ranch? But why was I getting worked up over their problems? Laura had made it very clear that she had no use for me.

At the moment, there was a worried look on her face. Noticing my attention, she straightened her back and looked ahead. From the tightening of her jaw, I figured she was mad. Chuckling, I turned my attention to my driving, and I asked Kitty how much farther we had to go.

"We'll be on our range in a few minutes," she said. "Then it's only a mile up to the house."

Kitty seemed to take great pride in their ranch, but Laura remained impassive. To pass the time, I chatted with Kitty until we reached the house.

I call it a house because Kitty did. Looking at it, I decided it surely didn't deserve the name. Cabin, or even shack, would be more fitting. Whoever built the house didn't know much about what he was doing. It was a thrown-together pile, and how it even stood was beyond me. None of the logs fit like they should, and the roof was merely a wagon cover thrown over some poles. I could see why Laura wasn't impressed with the place.

The house was even built in the wrong spot. The house and stable were set in a bowllike depression beside a small stream. After a rain, the water would pool up around the house. I'd be surprised if it didn't run through the front door every once in a while. And being slightly east of the stable, the house would be downwind of both the stable and the corrals.

Switching my attention to the stables, I saw that they also needed work, as did the corrals. The only thing that wasn't slipshod was the garden, which was large and green.

After pulling up the wagon in front of the house, I started carrying in the supplies. The inside of the cabin looked much like I had expected. A kitchen and living room made up the front part of the house. The back, partitioned off with a blanket, was sleeping quarters for the women, I reckoned.

On my third trip, I heard a man's voice call weakly from behind the blankets, and then, out of the corner of my eye, I saw Kitty and Laura exchange scared looks.

"You got company?" I asked slowly.

"No, that's our brother, Dickie," Laura said.

"He's been shot!" Kitty added.

Now I knew why Laura hadn't wanted me out here. "Was it Garland Chase?" I asked, dumping a sack of flour into the cupboard.

"No, Barry Ferriss," Kitty answered. "Ketchum has a bunch of men working for him, but Chase and Ferriss are by far the worst."

Something clicked in my brain when I

heard the name Ferriss. Somewhere I'd heard that name before. It wasn't anything I could put my finger on, just a shadow in my mind. Putting that aside, I stepped behind the curtain to have a look at the young man. And young he was, about a year or two younger than Laura, and slightly older than Kitty. He was a fine-looking lad too.

His wound was low down on the left side, and inflamed. My face hardened as I noted the position; it was clear that he had been shot from behind.

"This is infected. Did you have a doctor look at it?"

"How could we?" Laura cried. "If they knew he was still alive, they'd come back and finish the job!"

Now I understood her bitterness, and I said, "I'll see what I can do for him."

By the last light of the summer's day, I scouted around the fields for the herbs that Indians use to treat wounds.

Kitty had followed me out of the house, and she asked, "How bad is he? Will he be all right?"

"I've seen men live through worse. Depends on how strong he is." After a while I asked, "Where does this Ferriss figure in?"

"He works for Ketchum," she replied.

"Why does Ketchum want this ranch?"

"I'm not sure," Kitty said, a puzzled look coming over her pretty face. "But it's not just the ranch, because there's better places."

That followed my own line of thinking, but I hadn't expected such clever reasoning from someone so young, maybe only sixteen.

"Why don't you shave, Mr. Becker?" she asked suddenly. "You'd be so handsome."

Startled, I looked up and saw her moving up to me. "Do you think I'm pretty?" she asked.

"Why sure, you're real pretty," I said, taking a step back.

"Would you like to kiss me?" she asked with a taunting smile.

Even though most of the heat was gone from the day, I was sweating. "You're too young to be talking like that," I said roughly, trying to look stern and fatherly.

"Well, how else am I to meet a man out here?" she asked innocently.

"How the heck should I know? Ask your sister. She looks like she would know about such things." I took my hat off and wiped the sweat from my eyes.

"Oh, so you got eyes for Laura," Kitty said with a knowing look.

"No, I don't," I said, turning my hat in my hands. "It's getting dark, and you'd best go up to the house."

Laughing, she went back up to the house. It seemed like I always had more trouble than I could deal with. The last thing I needed was some starry-eyed little girl makin' up to me. Well, maybe she wasn't so little. Many girls her age were already married, or at least thinking about it.

I wiped the sweat from my forehead and resumed my search for the Indian herbs. Soon it was too dark to see, and I gave up and went back to the house.

Kitty wasn't in sight when I returned.

She was probably in her room, which suited me fine.

After hanging my hat by the door, I went to the stove and stoked the fire. From a handy bucket, I filled a pan with water and set it on the stove.

Laura was sitting beside her brother when I entered the other part of the house. "Can you really help him?" she asked skeptically.

I guess that my appearance didn't inspire much confidence. The sun and my sweat had faded my ragged blue shirt. Not even a bucket of polish could help my scarred boots. My entire body was covered with trail dust and I needed a shave and a haircut.

"I'll see what I can do," I said. "I've seen a lot of fellers shot, and mostly it depends on how much they want to live. Some die real easy, but I've seen fellers you couldn't kill with a cannon." Kneeling down, I looked at the wound. "Is the bullet still in there?"

"No, I took it out," Laura answered quietly.

Now, that set me back some. I didn't

figure she had the stomach for something like that, and I said so. She gave me a superior look and started to leave, but my voice stopped her: "Do you have any whiskey in the house, ma'am?"

"Of course not! We do not drink, Mr. Becker!" she snapped.

This brought a smile to my face as I drawled, "Knew some folks that didn't partake. Still, they was good folks. Anyway, whiskey is a good concoction to have around. Besides being a good painkiller, it's about the best antiseptic you can find. Shoot, I even knew a man who claimed it was good for snakebite."

She turned red under the sting of my words. Mad or not, she managed to keep her voice calm and even as she answered, "Well, I'm sorry, but we don't have any."

"That's okay. I keep a bottle in my saddlebag."

"You would!"

"Do you want to get it for me?"

It was clear by the way she pursed her lips that she did not, but she went anyway. I realized that I should be ashamed of myself for making fun of her, but the truth was, I enjoyed teasing her.

In a few minutes she returned with the bottle, and just to anger her, I took a healthy slug.

She shook her head and snapped at me, "Really, Mr. Becker!"

Grinning, I went past her into the kitchen and got the pan of water. I bathed the wound gently with the warm water. The bandage was stuck to the wound with dried blood, and I had to loosen the blood with hot water and be real careful as I peeled it off.

With liberal squirts of the whiskey I disinfected the wound. Afterward, I bandaged the wound loosely with a clean cloth that Laura provided.

Without giving Laura time to thank me, I went out and resumed unloading the wagon. When the job was finished, I drove the wagon down to the barn and unhitched the horses. After leading them and my horse inside, I took the saddle off the roan. The only feed I could find was some moldy hay. The McCray horses ate

it fine, but my contrary roan just turned
up his nose.

I stopped at the horse trough to wash
up some, and then I went on up to the
house. Kitty was setting the table while
Laura stirred something in a big pot.
After telling me to take a seat, Laura
filled my bowl with some kind of stew.

I wasn't sure what the stew was made
from, but long ago I'd learned not to ask.
Most times it's best not to know what
folks put in their stew—if you plan on
eating it, that is. My attempts to start a
conversation died immediately. Both
girls were lost in their own thoughts, so
I gave up and ate in silence. The stew
tasted delicious, but I didn't want to
admit it to that redheaded woman. I was
feeling a resentment toward her, and I'd
be danged if I'd compliment her about
her stew or anything else. If she asked,
I was prepared to say it was edible if you
were hungry. When she didn't ask, I was
a bit disappointed. She just toyed with her
own food, keeping her head down. I was
beginning to feel guilty about the way I
had treated her.

Feeling uncomfortable, I pushed back my plate, went outside, and lit a smoke. I knew it wasn't a good idea to light a cigarette after dark, but that woman had upset me some and I wasn't thinking. I've seen times when a man would get an arrow through his neck for smoking at night.

While standing by the door, I could hear the women talking inside. Not that I tried to listen in, but I couldn't help it.

"Well, what did you think of him?" Kitty asked.

"He's crude and vulgar. Why, he didn't even thank us for dinner!"

What! I didn't notice Laura blowing me any kisses for unloading her danged wagon. And it was a durned big wagon too. I had a notion to go in there and give her a piece of my mind.

"I like him," Kitty said.

"He's the most exasperating man I ever met," Laura snapped.

Exasperating? She was a fine one to talk! That woman could drive a bear from a cave. I heard Kitty laugh, and it was a pleasant sound.

"But there *is* something comforting about having him around," Laura admitted. "For the first time since we came here, I feel safe. He certainly handled those two men this morning."

I crushed out my smoke, stepped off the porch, and scouted around the place for a spot to bed down. I wore a smile, and I found myself wishing I had whupped the tar out of those two fellers that morning.

Chapter Two

As usual, I awoke just as the first streaks of light broke across the eastern sky. Like always, I took a moment to admire the sunrise. I had seen countless sunrises, but I still wondered at their beauty. Each one was slightly different from any other.

After putting away my bedroll, I threw my saddle on that ugly roan horse and led him from the barn. I usually wake up in a good mood, but not that horse of mine. In the morning he's as cantankerous as all get-out, and I always have to show him who's boss.

Today was no different and we had quite a set-to, but after he settled down, I began to scout the place. It wasn't a bad ranch, but it sure needed a lot more work than two skinny women could do. That Laura now, she wasn't really skinny. She had a lot in places where it could do the most good.

Pushing that thought from my mind, I rode full circle around the buildings. The stream wasn't deep, not more than a foot or so, but it was swift running and would carry a good bit of water. Running over the rocks the way it did, the water would be cold and pure.

The stream solved their water problem, but the grass close to the house was already growing thin. Buffalo grass such as this could only be grazed down so far before it began to die out, and they were going to have to claim more range. If they grazed this any lower, the dirt would start to blow, and once the ground started blowing in this country, you had to wait for a wet year for the grass to fill back in. Wet years in this country were mighty hard to come by.

Claiming more range was usually no problem. The way most ranchers did it was to move their cattle onto the range they wanted and lay claim to it. Trouble was, someone else might try to push your cattle out and take it for his own.

Once satisfied that no one was creeping around, I went back down to the house. The woodpile by the back door was growing thin, so I decided to replenish it.

Someone, probably the gals' brother, had dragged up some big logs behind the barn. They were just rotting there, and somebody had to chop them up and stack them by the kitchen door. Making up my mind to do it, I took up the ax and got with it.

After a couple of strokes, I stopped and looked at the blade on the ax, which was about as sharp as a marble. Mumblin' a bit, I hunted for a sandstone. One thing I couldn't abide was a dull ax. Finding a stone that would serve my purpose, I put an edge on the ax that you could shave with.

As I worked, I smiled, recalling how my pa used to beat me to get me up and at the woodpile. And here I was doing it without even being asked. Shows what the sight of a pretty woman will do to a man.

After about an hour, I saw smoke rising from the chimney and knew that somebody was up and about inside. After washing up in the horse trough, I scraped my hand across my beard and then decided to shave.

When I went inside, both women were scuttling around the stove. They both looked at me a little surprised. Kitty smiled a little, and Laura said, "I see you finally cleaned up. Last night you didn't look human."

This was the most exasperating woman I had ever met. I had spent half the night unloading her supplies, and then had gotten up and chopped wood, but she still had the gall to chew me out.

"I told you he was handsome," Kitty said brightly.

"Kitty! You shouldn't talk like that," Laura scolded.

Having been born with good sense, I stayed out of that and ducked into a handy chair. "How's the boy doing this morning?" I asked.

"He's better, thank you," Laura answered stiffly.

"Are you going to stay for a while and help us?" Kitty asked in her direct way.

"Kitty, I'm sure Mr. Becker has better things to do," Laura said. "I'm positive we can do all that needs to be done," she added.

I snorted and swore a little over that one. "Ma'am," I went on, "there's more work here that needs to be done right now than you two could do in a year."

"Do not raise your voice in my house!" Laura snapped.

Kitty was laughing at us. I started to cuss, then remembered Laura and stopped. Swallowing those words, I grabbed my coffee cup. Now let me tell you, when those ladies set a cup of coffee on the table, it's just off the boil. So when I took a big gulp, it felt like I'd just swallowed a handful of branding irons. My mouth got scalded all through, and it burned my lips some.

I swore without thinking, and was immediately sorry. The look that came into Laura's green eyes put gray hairs on my head. Kitty was openly laughing now, and that made me even madder. "Where's my whiskey?" I asked, suddenly feeling the need for a drink.

"I poured it out last night," Laura said, all high and mighty.

If I was a little peeved before, I was mad plumb through by now. "You *what?*" I screamed, lunging to my feet. I banged my knee on the underside of the table, but I paid it no mind, and I roared, "Woman, I ought to—"

"If you do not calm down, I'll have to ask you to leave," Laura threatened.

"Don't bother, I'm leaving right now!" I thundered.

Kitty was about to keel over from laughing so hard, which upset me even more. Now, a man ought not lose his head like I was doing. First thing you know, he goes and does something stupid. Which was just what I did.

This morning, when I dismounted, I did what I always did and loosened the cinch on my saddle. Mad as I was right now, I plumb forgot about it, but not for long. I put a boot in the stirrup and started to swing up. The next thing I knew I was lying in the dirt and that horse was looking down at me with that disgusted look he had. Seemed like he was sidin' with them women.

Oh, they'd seen it all right. They stood on the porch hacking and laughing like they were going to have a stroke, which was what I hoped for.

Red-faced, I resaddled and rode out of there like the devil was chasing me. A mile down the road, I was still madder than a stepped-on snake. I cussed Kitty and my horse, but most of all I cussed that green-eyed, redheaded witch-woman.

I had never considered myself an easily angered man, but since meeting that woman, it seemed that all I did was fuss and fume. And all that fussing was working me into a froth.

The nerve of that woman! I had a notion to go back and give her a piece of my mind. Durned right I would.

Without thinking, I jerked the head of that horse around. That roan and I had been together quite a spell, and we'd reached an agreement. He let me ride him as long as I showed him a proper respect. We were trotting along just fine when I jerked his head like that. Well, sir, the next moment I found myself in the dust. Again!

Just like before, that horse stared down at me like I was stupid. Which was just how I felt. I was mighty sore, but my good sense was coming back.

Calmer now, I crawled back in the middle of that horse and headed for town. To heck with her. I leaned back in the saddle and rolled a smoke, which soothed my nerves some. The smoke and the nice morning helped to bring back my normal good humor, and I began to enjoy the ride.

A little later, I noticed a dust cloud coming my way. The only thing to raise a cloud of dust like that would be a bunch of riders, a big bunch. Being a careful man by nature, I like to look folks over before they see me. And after this morning, I was inclined to be doubly cautious.

Back down the trail a ways, I had noticed a draw that would hide both me and my horse. Turning that roan gently around, I made my way back there. This was a well-used trail, so I wasn't worried about their seeing my tracks. A good tracker could sort them out, but I didn't figure these hombres would be paying that close attention.

I turned the roan in the draw, which he didn't care for, not that I blamed him. The air was hot and heavy in there. I dismounted and led him well back out of sight. Then I went back to the mouth of the draw and sifted some dust over the tracks where I'd turned off the trail. Bellying down behind a rock, I waited for them to come.

In a few minutes they came riding into sight. One look was all I needed to tell that this was trouble, real trouble. One of them had a kerosene can tied behind his saddle, and they were headed right for the McCray place. It looked to me like Ketchum had gotten tired of playing around and had decided to burn the McCrays out.

I sized them up carefully, but didn't see Garland Chase. Still, I was sure they were Ketchum's men. Maybe Chase didn't want to come. I'd heard that he was a fighting man, and this wouldn't be his style.

For a moment, I even contemplated going back, but then I remembered that my help wasn't needed or even wanted. Anyway, if this bunch was going to tackle that redheaded woman head-on, I felt sorry for them.

As I sat there watching those riders file by, I convinced myself that the McCrays and their problems were none of my business. So when those riders disappeared from sight, I resumed my journey for town.

"Aw shoot!" I groaned after going only a few yards. I was going back and I knew it. It just wasn't in me to let two women face their problems alone.

Giving the riders enough slack so they wouldn't see me, I followed along. While they dismounted in front of the house, I slipped closer and slid down behind a fallen log.

They left one man to hold the horses, and then they spread out and advanced on the house. I wondered about their method of attack. A good rifleman inside the house could have shortened their numbers in a hurry, but I guess they didn't figure to have any trouble with two women. Of course, they didn't know those two like I did.

From where I lay, I couldn't make out all of what was said, but they seemed to be ordering the McCrays off. Kitty was nowhere to be seen, but Laura was out there facing up to them. One thing I had to give that woman credit for—she had spunk. A lot of it.

I considered letting that redheaded woman run them off by herself, but these boys didn't deserve that kind of shame. It occurred to me to shoot the kerosene can one of them was holding, but I might miss the can and hit Laura. It's been my experience that stopping a bullet worsens a person's disposition, and Laura surely didn't need that. She was already meaner than a grizzly bear.

Just then, I had a good idea. The man holding the horse wore spurs with big Mexican-style rowels. Sliding my rifle across the top of the log, I drew a bead on one of those spurs. I squeezed off my shot and laughed as he spun around and lit on his behind. Crying out in pain, he let loose of the reins and grabbed his leg.

Next, I put a bullet in the sand in front of the horses. They did just what I had hoped, and took out of there. The two quick shots and the gravel spitting in their faces really spooked them. They would run clear home, I reckoned.

Swinging my rifle back to cover those gents in the yard, I said conversationally, "If I was you, I'd stand real still." I waited a second, then added slyly, "Unless a bunch of you want to cash in your chips right now."

I never saw so many still hombres in all my life, especially when a rifle barrel poked around the edge of a curtain. It was so quiet that I could hear the lever being worked, as by somebody getting ready to fire.

All of a sudden, those boys noticed what I'd seen earlier. Spread out in the open, they made good targets, being a good twenty yards to the nearest cover. But to them, I imagine, it looked a lot farther. It was a cinch bet that some of them would never make it.

I let them stand and contemplate a minute. Then I made a suggestion: "If you boys figure on being home for supper, you'd best start now. But it appears like you're gonna have to walk, 'cause something spooked your horses."

Oh, they did some grumbling, but they started down the trail. These boys were paid fighting men, but they didn't figure to lose any hide earning their pay.

I let them walk a ways before I stopped them and said, "You boys got a long walk ahead of you, so it don't make no sense to be packing all that hardware." They surely didn't want to leave their guns, but I had the drop on them. Seeing them hesitate, I prodded them a mite: "Drop them guns or use them. Makes no difference to me."

Slowly, one by one, they dropped their guns in the dust and resumed walking. A burly, black-haired man—Ketchum, I reckoned—just had to mumble some tough talk before he left: "You just dug your own grave, friend."

I paid him no attention. I was too busy trying to pick out Ferriss. When I spotted him, I knew him instantly. He was a short man with a cold, still face, the kind of face that would make you shiver every time you saw it. Like a rattler, swift and deadly—that's what this gent would be.

I watched them till they were out of sight. The one whose spur I'd shot was limping badly. If I was any judge, he had a badly wrenched knee, and the long walk home was going to do him no good.

Satisfied with a job well done, I went back to where I'd tied my horse. That ugly devil was chomping grass, paying no mind to humans and their strange doings. Ugly, stubborn, and contrary, he was still the best horse I'd ever owned, and he knew it too.

I mounted and rode down to the yard. That cantankerous redheaded woman stood with her hands on her hips, and I could tell she was mad. I had sort of thought that what I'd done might deserve a thank-you, but one look at her and I knew I just wasn't going to get it.

"You enjoyed that," she accused.

Well, to tell the truth, I guess I did. But what was wrong with that? It's bred into a man to enjoy a good fight, especially when he comes out the winner. When I said as much to her, she threw a fit.

"A *gentleman* doesn't," she informed me. "And a gentleman always thanks a lady when she cooks for him."

Being around her was like shaking hands with a porcupine. You were always getting jabbed and poked.

"I don't know what a gentleman does, but I figure a lady should thank a man for pulling her bacon out of the fire like I just did for you."

"I could have handled them."

"Maybe," I admitted. Chances are that she might have sent them packing, but these were tough boys. She might have handled them if Ferriss wasn't along, but with him present, she wouldn't have had a chance. Most of those boys would have a hard time shooting at a woman, but not Ferriss.

"Ma'am, whether you like it or not, you're gonna have to hire some help," I told her. "You can bet your petticoats them boys will be back, and next time they'll come ready for a scrap."

"But we don't have any money to hire help," Kitty said.

Startled, I jerked around to see her standing right behind me. I hadn't even noticed her come out of the house. An uneasy feeling came over me, kind of a chill running up and down my spine. It just naturally ain't healthy to have folks creeping up behind you. First thing you know, one of them slides a knife between your ribs.

"Western men may not have the manners of your Eastern gentlemen," I said tiredly, "but they don't need money to help a couple of ladies in trouble. And if they are pretty, like you two, so much the better."

Laura's face softened a mite, and I noticed that when she wasn't mad, she was a good-looking woman. When that thought hit home, I felt sort of panicky.

"But I thought we whipped them," Kitty said.

"No, them boys are poker players," I told her. "They know that when you ain't got the cards, you toss in your hand and wait for a new shuffle."

"Mr. Becker, could you look in on Dickie?" Laura asked in a sweet tone.

I nodded and followed her into the house. Behind the curtain, Dickie was awake, and he felt a bunch better. As easy as I could, I took off the bandage. The wound looked better and was beginning to scab over. Some of the redness was gone, and the swelling had eased a bit.

While I worked, Kitty told him how I had helped, and that I was going to get more men.

He thanked me, then added, "Wish I could help."

I waved off his thanks and told him, "You just get well." I liked this kid and felt sorry for him too. Being shot was bad enough, but to be cooped up with these two women? I shuddered at the thought of it.

Turning from the bed, I saw Laura at the curtain, watching me with a funny look on her pretty face.

"Don't bandage that till tonight. The

fresh air and sunlight will do it good," I explained.

In the kitchen, after pouring myself a cup of coffee, I laid out my plans to the women. "I figure to ride into that town and send a wire. What's the name of that town?" I asked, realizing I didn't know.

"Cordell," Kitty said.

"If I ride hard, I can get around them fellers and slip into town." I raised my cup to my lips and took a careful sip. They were both staring at me, and it made me most uncomfortable. They reminded me of a cat watching a bird. "Well, I best be getting off," I said.

At the door, I stopped and sneaked a peek back. Laura was still watching me. I couldn't tell what she was thinking, but she looked kind of soft around the mouth, like she was about to smile. Also, her eyes looked kind of dreamy. I opened the door and scooted out to my horse. Him I understood. He was mean and contrary. He'd kick me if he got the chance and bite me if I wasn't careful. Come to think of it, he reminded me of Laura.

I had always had the feeling that that

horse was laughing up his sleeve at me. Whenever I was around Laura, I got the same feeling. It was enough to give a man the willies.

Chapter Three

When I was a mile down the road, that hot, trapped feeling began to fade. About half-way to town, I eased by Ketchum's men, and just for fun, I raised some dust by shooting in among them. The sight of them scrambling for cover kept me laughing for a mile or so.

I stopped laughing, though, when I saw the body lying in the trail ahead. Shucking my Winchester, I scouted around a bit before I approached it. Even before getting down, I could tell it was Garland Chase. I looped the reins around the pommel and stepped down. He was alive. The two bullets in his chest were high enough to have missed his heart.

Though he was barely conscious, I asked him about the shooting.

"It was that devil Ferriss. I tried to

stop them. I tried. . . ." He passed out from the effort of speaking.

Knowing that those men were not far behind, I didn't take time to look at his wounds, I just put him on my horse. For once, that horse didn't give me any problems. Perhaps he knew that I was in no mood for trifling.

Once I was up behind Chase, I faced up to my problem. What the devil was I going to do with him? It was a safe bet that if I took him to town, Ketchum's men would finish him off. About the only thing I could do was take him to the Mc-Cray place. This meant I wouldn't get my wire sent, but I couldn't help that now.

It was a long ride and Chase was a heavy man. My arms ached something fierce by the time I got there. The women came out of the cabin and asked all kinds of questions. When I asked them to help me get him down, Laura got as balky as a mule.

"Have you forgotten who this is?" she asked coldly.

"That's Garland Chase, our enemy," Kitty pointed out.

Sometimes a man can just plain lose patience, and I did that now. "Would you shut up and help me?" I guess I was roaring like a wounded bear, but like I said, sometimes a man can run out of patience.

Maybe it was my bellowing, or maybe they finally came to their senses, but for once, they quit exercising their jaws and helped.

It was a struggle, but we got him down without dropping him and carried him into their bedroom. It was the first time I had been in this part of the house, and it looked about what I expected—neat as a tack. It didn't even look like anyone lived in it. A room should have a lived-in look, so's a body can tell something about the person who sleeps there.

"Be nice to have some liquor to clean these wounds with, but somebody poured it out," I commented sarcastically.

Laura's head snapped up, and she stuck her chin out. "I'm sorry you don't have anything to clean his wound with, but I'm not sorry I poured it out. You probably would have gotten drunk last night if I hadn't."

"That's okay. I got two more bottles in my other saddlebag," I said, grinning.

Laura's face turned pale, and she gave me that look again, but she made no sound.

While Kitty went to fetch the whiskey, Laura asked if there was anything she could do to help. "You could help me get his pants off," I suggested.

Well, I was somewhat disappointed. I had figured she would raise hob with that, but she didn't. Together, we rassled his jeans off, and with my knife I slit his long underwear. It always did beat me why some fellers wear long underwear all summer.

The wound didn't look much like a bullet wound. The skin was laid open like it had been done with a knife. Kitty returned with the whiskey, and if it bothered her to see a man in his underwear, she didn't show it.

"Have you got any thread?" I asked.

"You mean like to sew with?" Laura asked.

"I don't know of any other kind," I replied cheerfully. "Bring a needle too," I called after her.

After dousing the wound in whiskey, I took the needle and thread from Laura. Then, with a skill picked up over the years, I closed the wound.

"You look like you've done that before," Kitty commented.

"Yeah, I've sewed up a few folks, myself included," I replied with a bit of pride.

"You gave yourself stitches?" Laura asked, arching her eyebrows.

"When you're out on the range, it ain't often that there's anybody around to help you."

With Chase's leg taken care of, I looked at his chest and was pleased to find that both bullets had gone plumb through. I never was any hand at probing for slugs.

Using the whiskey, I cleaned both wounds, which were so close together that they formed almost one hole. They went in right under the collarbone and came out the top of the shoulder in the back. They would be sore, but once he got over the shock of losing blood, I figured that Chase would be fine.

Once the wounds were clean, I went into the kitchen and got a handful of flour. Under the disbelieving looks of the two women, I packed the wound with flour and bandaged it tight. "Helps to stop the bleeding," I said. "I'm sure he'll make it. When he wakes up, give him salt mixed in water. It'll help make up for the blood he lost."

"I don't see why you're so worried about him. He's one of Ketchum's men," Kitty said.

"No, he broke with them. Fact is, Barry Ferriss is the one who shot him."

From the blank looks on their faces, I could tell they didn't know what I meant.

"He'll be switching sides. Men like Chase don't like being shot at," I said, spelling it out for them. "And he can't afford to set quiet now."

"Why is that?" Kitty asked.

"Chase has a reputation of being a good man with a gun. That's how he earns a living. If word gets out that Ferriss beat him, Chase won't be able to find a job, to say nothing of the punks who'll come looking for him."

Having said my piece, I went to my horse. I wanted to see how Ketchum and his boys were faring. I had one foot in the stirrup when I remembered that the horses in the barn had to be fed.

As I forked hay to them, I reminded myself to turn them out in the morning. Poor as it was, we'd need what little hay was left if Ketchum attacked, and I was certain he would. And next time he would come loaded for a long and final attack.

I caught up with the walking men as the last bit of daylight faded from the sky. They looked hot, dusty, and, from their grumbling, I'd say they were in a black mood. The first place they headed was to the saloon for a drink.

Once they were all inside, I tied up the roan and cat-footed up to the back of the saloon. Even with the window closed, I could hear Ketchum ranting and raving. With the point of my knife, I eased the window open.

"Nobody takes my gun and sends me packing. Do you hear me? Nobody!" Ketchum shouted. He grabbed a beer from the bartender before he had the glass filled. He took a long drink, spilling half of it down his shirt. He came up spitting and sputtering. "Get some guns. We're going back out there!" he roared, throwing the glass aside.

"I don't think that would be wise, Mr. Ketchum," a cool voice said. The speaker was a wiry man with an untidy shock of blond hair. He looked to be a hillbilly, probably from Tennessee or Arkansas. Wherever he was from, he seemed like a cool character.

This guy and Ferriss were the only men in the room with guns. The others had been more interested in getting a drink, but these two had armed themselves first.

Ketchum bowed his head and hunched his shoulders. He reminded me of a bull about to charge. "What do you mean, Murdock?" he asked the hillbilly.

"They'll be ready now. It'd be best to wait a few days. Let all the watching and worrying wear them down."

Murdock would bear watching. Without him, Ketchum could be prodded into doing something stupid. I'd heard of Murdock. He had drifted out from Tennessee and hired to the big outfits as a fighting man. And from what I'd heard, he earned his pay. Though not a fast-draw expert like Ferriss, Murdock got results. When he had a man to kill, Murdock killed him, usually at long range with that big Sharps he carried. That Sharps shot a .50 caliber bullet, which would stack up favorably with a cannonball.

I could see that Ketchum was considering Murdock's suggestion, and so was Barry Ferriss. Ferriss had been prowling the room like a caged panther. "No!" he screamed. "Why mess around? Let's go out there now. I'll call Becker out and kill him!" Ferriss bellowed, slapping his hand to his gun.

Suddenly, I had a strong notion to go in there and give him his chance. If I'd been sure that Murdock would stay out of it, I would have too.

"I don't think Becker would be fool

enough to come out of the house," Murdock said. "Even if he beat Ferriss, we would have him."

Ferriss froze in his tracks, and even from outside I could feel the tension settle over the room. For a long time Ferriss stared at Murdock.

"You don't think I can take Becker?" Ferriss asked, his voice so low I could barely hear it.

Murdock didn't answer. He just sat on a card table and watched Ferriss. Murdock didn't say anything, but his rifle spoke a silent warning to Ferriss. Ferriss didn't seem to notice the rifle pointed at his stomach. I could see his hand inching toward his gun, and for a minute I thought he would draw. But then I saw his eyes widen and freeze on Murdock's rifle.

"Finally got around to noticing, did you?" Murdock commented. His sly smile gave me the impression that he would enjoy killing Ferriss.

My legs cramped from kneeling so long. As I shifted my position, my foot struck a discarded bottle and knocked it over. Before I could even blink, Ferriss wheeled and snapped two shots at the window. Man, he was quick! I felt a whiff of air as the bullets screamed past my head.

Ducking low, I scrambled for my horse. Behind me, I could hear the shouts and curses of Ketchum's men as they tried to organize a pursuit.

Out of breath, I reached the roan and vaulted into the saddle. Instead of heading for the McCray ranch, I circled the town, and from behind the general store, I watched the street. Ketchum's men ran back and forth, trying to round up guns and horses. I didn't see Ferriss, and that worried me. The man was a little off his rocker, and there wasn't any guessing what he might do. Crazy or not, he was quick and dangerous. I shuddered at the thought of facing him.

Then I spotted him leaning against the wall of the saloon. He had a bottle in one hand and didn't look to be in any hurry to get a horse and give chase. I guess chasing around in the dark for an armed man didn't appeal to him.

I could see Ketchum and Murdock holding a powwow in the middle of the street. Murdock seemed to be explaining something to the big rancher. Ketchum nodded a couple of times, and Murdock walked down to the stable.

I didn't want to be on the road with Murdock prowling around, so I turned the roan toward home. I would have given my bottom dollar to know what Murdock had told Ketchum. I had a feeling my life could depend on it.

Supper was on the table and waiting by the time I put the roan up for the night. I didn't eat with much appetite, though. I kept picturing Ferriss turning and firing. To tell the truth, I wondered if I could match his speed.

After supper I looked in on my patients. Dickie was awake and restless. After talking a spell, he asked the very question that had been troubling me: "What I can't figure is why Ketchum wants this place so bad. There are better places around, and most of them are closer to his home range."

What Dickie said made sense. Why

would a man bother to take land that was plumb on the other side of town from his holdings? While Dickie talked, an idea came to me, and I told him, "Maybe he don't especially want your place. Maybe he just hates you."

"I don't see how he could. I've never met the man," Dickie declared.

Now that made things even more puzzling. "You get some rest. I'm gonna check in on Chase," I said.

Chase was awake when I entered his room. "Never thought you'd pick me up, but I'm glad you did. Thanks." I waved off his thanks and asked how he was feeling. "Pretty good, but my shoulder feels like it's on fire."

"Must be the whiskey I used to clean it," I commented solemnly.

He lay silent for a while, then asked, "Where am I?" When I told him, he looked relieved. "What I figured. I take it you held them off."

"Yeah, we caught them out in the open and they didn't make an issue of it. Why did they shoot you?"

"Well, now, I didn't hold with the

whole deal. I didn't like scaring the women, but I done it. I didn't care for sending Ferriss to kill that boy. If I had known about that, I would've stopped it." He paused for a moment, then added, "Maybe I would have tried."

I believed Chase. He sounded sincere. I'd heard of him, a real fighting man. His kind wouldn't go in for murdering women and kids. I decided to relieve some of his guilt.

"Appears to me that Ketchum needs to get himself a new gun hand." When Chase looked confused, I explained. "Ferriss didn't kill you, and he didn't kill that boy, either."

Chase gripped my arm with enough strength to rassle bears. His eyes bright and shiny, he demanded, "What do you mean?"

"Well, the kid is in the next room, and he's in better shape than you."

Chase fell back in the bed and relaxed. I could tell that the news had taken a load off his mind.

"Don't low-rate the man," Chase cautioned. "He's as fast as lightning. I made a mistake. I was watching Ketchum when I should have been looking out for Ferriss."

"He's fast all right, maybe too fast for his own good. Looks like he shot before his gun got good and level," I said, pointing to his bandaged leg.

Chase's face sobered as he told me what had happened. "Ketchum knew that I would never stand for burning out those women, so he sent me off after some horses. But I knew what they were about, so I circled around and cut them off outside of town. When I braced Ketchum . . . well, Ferriss dealt himself in. I should have been watching the little weasel, but I figured the others would back off," Chase continued with a touch of bitterness. "Ferriss always hated me, and when he saw his chance, he horned in."

Chase was getting tired, so I rose to leave. At the curtain I stopped. "One more thing—do you have any idea why Ketchum wants this place so bad?"

Chase looked funny as he answered. "Now, there's a question. I've been won-

dering about that myself. At first I figured he wanted one of the women. But
now. . . ." Chase's words trailed off as he
ran out of ideas.

Chapter Four

The next morning I awoke and went in for a breakfast that was a sight more friendly than the day before. Still, I kept my head down and ate with as little fuss as possible. The last thing I wanted this morning was to set off Laura. After thanking them for the meal, I went down to the barn to turn the horses out to graze.

On my way to the barn I scanned the tree line. I was almost to the barn door when a skunk ran out almost under my feet. Quickly, I did the natural thing and turned to get my behind out of there. But when I lunged, I clean forgot about the horse trough behind me. I banged into it and ended up sprawled in the mud on the other side.

I reckon I was lucky that I didn't land in the trough, but right then I didn't feel real lucky. After a brief inspection, I found that except for a couple of barked-up shins I was all right.

To make matters worse, I looked up to see that redheaded woman shaking her head on the porch. She didn't laugh, but I bet she wanted to. I got off the ground acussin' and as mad as I could be, but by the time I had the horses staked out, I had cooled down some, and I even chuckled as I recalled how funny my shenanigan must have looked.

Wanting to stick close to the ranch today, I ambled over to the little stand of trees I'd noticed earlier. After pacing it off, I saw that the clearing between the trees was just about the right size for a house.

Using a shovel, I leveled up the ground, and afterward I scouted the creek for some flat stones. I carried the ones I wanted to the spot where I'd marked out the floor. I toted quite a few stones before deciding I'd had enough for now. After dinner I would use the buckboard and get some more.

Since I'd helped lay a few stone floors in my time, I had an idea how to do it.

Picking the right stones and laying them so that they fit close and level took some skill. While not the best of house builders maybe, I did a fair job.

Sweat rolled down my back and chest, but I enjoyed the work. It was good for a man to do a little hard work every once in a while. As long as he didn't get carried away and make it a habit.

Pretty soon, Laura came up to see what I was doing, and I told her, "Your house is built in the wrong spot. Here you'll be cooler in the summer and warmer in the winter."

She looked surprised. I bet she would never have guessed I worried about such things. She probably thought that all I cared about were horses and guns. I had given some thought to having a home, but I could tell she thought I was just a drifting cowboy, bent on drinking and generally raising the devil.

"Why are you building the floor?" she asked.

"Never was one to just sit about. I figure Ketchum will try again, and I should be close." I showed her the outline of the house, and said that if a porch was built on the back, it would be a nice place to sit on summer evenings. "And that would be a nice place to put a flower garden," I went on, pointing to a spot just south of where the front door would be.

Laura admitted it would be a good spot, but she still had to argue: "Yes, I suppose so, but I don't have any seeds."

"There's some wildflowers in them hills yonder. When this here trouble is over, if you want, I'll take you up there. We could transplant some."

"That would be nice, Mr. Becker. Now let's go eat," she said, taking my arm.

All of a sudden I began to sweat, and that old trapped feeling crept up on me. I felt like running for those far-off hills, but I swallowed hard and stayed put. Growing distrustful of her good mood, I figured it was too good to last, and I was right on target.

When we entered the house arm in arm like that, Kitty gave us a curious look. It was about then that the lid blew off.

"Mr. Becker, don't you ever wipe your feet?" Laura flared.

Well, I looked back and, sure enough, there were two little pieces of dried mud, which was nothing to get excited about. The way she screeched and carried on, you'd think that I'd dragged in the whole Arkansas River bottom.

Having learned better than to argue, I picked up the mud and threw it outside. While out there, I cleaned my boots and tried to put a rein on my temper. Shoot, how'd a man have time to clean his boots with her dragging him in the door like that?

When I came back in, Dickie was sitting at the table, and Laura turned to me and ordered, "Tell him to get back into bed."

"Aw, let him be. Getting up and around could be the best thing for him," I said, mainly to oppose her, but then I cautioned Dickie to go easy: "Don't go and bust that wound open."

As usual, the food tasted mighty good, and I ate with a good appetite, which was surprising, considering the situation. Now and again, when I dared, I'd sneak a peek across the table. Laura was glaring at me like she wished me harm. By now, I knew that those looks wouldn't hurt me, so I paid 'em no mind.

After dinner I helped Dickie out to the porch, where it would do him good to sit in the sun. Then, feeling stuffed and wishing to loaf for a bit, I went to check on Chase. I noticed that somebody had taken the blanket down from the window. I knew how he felt. Both of us were out-of-doors types, and being cooped up got on a body's nerves, but the sunlight and the breeze streaming through the window would help. He said to me with a sly smile, "Looks like you're getting house-broke. Are you thinking of getting married and settling down?"

I durn near plugged him for a crack like that. It must have showed in my eyes, 'cause he stopped laughing and turned serious.

"Seen any of Ketchum's men?" he asked. When I told him I hadn't, he gave me a stern warning: "They'll be back, and you can bet the farm on that. When they come, prop me up to that window and give me a gun."

I didn't argue with him, for I knew we would need him. So far we had been lucky, but I didn't figure it would last forever.

A worrisome feeling came on me later as I hooked up the buckboard. I almost wished they would attack and get it over with. For a moment I even thought of going into town and calling out Ketchum. But if I was killed, there would be no one to protect the women. Neither Chase nor Dickie was in any shape to put up much of a fight. No, the only thing I could do was wait.

I drove the wagon up on the ridge behind the house, and then began to load rocks for the floor. I'd been at it for about an hour when I saw Laura come out the side door. She had something in her hand that I recognized immediately. A whiskey bottle. *My* whiskey bottle.

With a tremendous roar, I ran down that slope bellowing like a bull stuck in the mud. Why, I must've been taking six or eight feet to the bound.

I didn't slow down for that little ole stream. I figured to step right in the middle and clear to the other side. Now in most places a body can cross that stream and it ain't more than a foot deep. So you can see why I was somewhat surprised when my foot settled on nothing but water, and I sank in over my head. I came up sputtering and a little out of breath.

Paying that no mind, I slipped and scrambled up to the bank. Falling once, I sloshed my way over to that witch-woman at about the time she started to pour. I snatched the bottle from her hand and took a long pull from it. Now I hadn't taken the time to notice what she was pouring from that bottle. After the first swig, well, I sat up and took notice. Whatever was in that bottle was scalding hot!

I tried to cuss, but it took me three tries to get the words out. "What in blue blazes was in that?" I demanded hoarsely.

"Water, silly," she said, and then added with a smile, "hot water."

Grumbling, I started to leave when an awful thought came to me. "What did you do with my whiskey?" I asked almost in a panic.

"Why, I poured it out," she said, and I let out a howl. "The other night," she added sweetly.

"Huh?" I said, more than a little confused.

"This is the bottle I poured out the other night. I was cleaning it so I could store things in it," she said all innocent-like.

I grumbled a little more under my breath. By Joe, one of these days I was gonna. . . .

"You shouldn't swear so much, Mr. Becker," she advised.

"Feller once told me that the reason mule skinners cuss so much is they gotta deal with ornery, stubborn mules all the time. At the time, I didn't see why that would make a body cuss, but now I reckon I understand."

Laura let that remark pass, but then she said, "You don't look hurt. Besides, you were needing a bath."

A bath! Who had time for a bath? Why, with folks shooting at me, I barely had time to eat. Well, maybe nobody had actually shot me, but they would have if I'd have let them.

As I sloshed back to the buckboard, I realized that it had been a few days since I'd had a bath. Since I was already wet, maybe now would be a good time. Yes sir, a bath would feel right nice just about now. Making up my mind to do it, I drove the wagon over to the barn.

Chapter Five

Drenched, I unhitched the buckboard and put the horses in the barn. After I had fed and watered all the horses, I dug into my saddlebag for my razor and soap. Then I grabbed the oak bucket and headed for the door.

That durned horse of mine kicked me when I passed behind him. That's right! He just reached out with a back leg and thumped me on the shin. Let me tell you, it smarted some, and being already in a surly mood, I took a swing at him with the bucket.

The way my luck had been going lately, you can probably guess what happened. That bucket hit one of those upright beams supporting the roof, bounced back, and whomped me on the jaw.

This time I didn't even cuss. What was the use? I just wobbled down to the creek, where a dip in the stream might help to clear the cobwebs out of my head. It also set me to thinking.

Now, I'd always spoofed at people who believed in haunts, witches, curses, and the like, but now I was wondering. It sure did seem like that green-eyed, redheaded woman had put a curse on me.

What I mean is, just look at what had happened to me. I'd been thrown from my horse twice—*twice* in one day!

Never in my life had I been thrown twice in the same *month.* I'd been smacked in the head with a bucket, durned near drowned in the creek, and had my mouth scalded till it felt like sandpaper. Yes sir, she hadn't taken to me from the start, and had piled a whole lot of grief on me.

Right then, I made up my mind to leave first thing in the morning. I wouldn't go to Cordell, but head south around it. The first town I came to, I'd stop and leave word. All I'd have to do is mention that two pretty and unmarried women were in trouble, and they'd have plenty of help by nightfall.

I felt slightly ashamed for letting that woman run me off, but I didn't let it change my mind. After all, she didn't seem to want me to stay, so why should I risk my life for her?

The dip in the stream felt good, and since I'd made my decision to leave, I began to relax. But I didn't relax so much that I forgot to keep an eye out for trouble. No sirree, I didn't trust that Ketchum outfit one bit. It would be just like them to try a sneak attack.

When I finally decided I was clean, I got out of the water and checked my clothes. They were mostly dry so I climbed into my jeans. After taking the bucket of water out of the sun where I'd left it to heat, I shaved and felt a lot better. Next, I gathered my gun belt, shrugged into my shirt, and headed up to the house.

On my way I noticed Laura working in the garden. I stopped to watch her and I liked the picture. She sure didn't look like a witch-woman now. Matter of fact, she looked like something out of a dream.

Why I did it I don't know, but I walked

right up to her. I mean, when a feller sees a bear on the trail, he usually gives it a wide berth. And believe me, this red-headed woman was meaner than any bear ever thought about being. I don't know. Maybe I wanted to show her that I wasn't a total slob.

"My, my, don't you look nice," she said, smiling.

Even though I had a sneaking suspicion that she was making fun of me, her words pleased me. "Thanks," I mumbled, a little embarrassed.

"You know, I think maybe Kitty was right. You *are* handsome. Of course, a haircut would help," she suggested slyly.

I supposed that it would, but I didn't have time to hunt up a barber. When I told her that, she volunteered to cut it.

"I cut Dickie's all the time," she assured me.

Against my better judgment, I let her talk me into the notion. I began to realize that she was always talking me into doing something I didn't care to do. I don't quite know how she did it, either.

"You go sit under that tree while I get

my scissors," she said. Though it sounded mighty like an order, she said it in such a sweet tone that I let it pass.

We talked pleasantly while she snipped away. I found out that when she wasn't rawhidin' a man, she was nice. I took a chance and asked how her family came to settle out here.

"We were born and raised in St. Louis. Our mother died when I was quite young. Our father owned a store, but Dickie had no taste for storekeeping, so when Father died, we sold out and came here."

"You don't like it here, do you?" I asked.

"I don't know. Kitty and Dickie love it. I used to hate it here, but now I'm not sure."

"I reckon folks here are a little crude for your taste," I commented without thinking.

Then I realized she might take that wrong, and she had a pair of scissors in her hand. It would be just like her to lop my ear off. Flinching, I rolled my eyes to where I could see her, but she appeared not to have even heard me. She had a faraway look like her mind was someplace else. Right now she didn't look like a witch-woman. Fact was, she looked mighty like an angel. I almost laughed at myself for being scared of this lovely young woman. Why, she wasn't near big enough to hurt even a fly. I'd bet she wouldn't weigh over a hundred pounds.

"I was being courted by a nice young man before we left." Her voice startled me out of my thoughts. "He was from one of the best families in St. Louis. He used to take me to the finest balls, and we would dine in the best restaurants. It was so grand. Everyone had such manners and style," she said dreamily.

Now I really felt miserable. For the past few minutes I'd been having tender thoughts about her, but I knew I could never compete with that fancy living in St. Louis. To tell the truth, I wasn't right sure what a ball was. I'd ask Garland Chase. He would know.

"No, I do not despise the people out here. It's just that they aren't . . . well . . . cultured."

I wasn't quite sure what cultured

meant, either. I reckoned it had something to do with the manners and style she spoke about.

"Ma'am, I know I ain't no gentleman, but there is a few of them around. Fact of the matter, you got one staying in your house right now," I told her.

"Who's that?" she asked skeptically.

"Garland Chase," I said, and watched the surprise come over her face. Before she could protest, I added, "He comes from one of those fancy plantations down south. Seems he might've killed a couple of fellers and had to hightail it out of there."

"But I've talked with him and he sounds just like you," she said.

I do declare that woman sure liked to argue. "He's just fitting in with the country. Most folks will get to talking like the folks around them. It's just a habit you pick up, I reckon." For a change she was quiet, and I let her consider for a moment. "I never did see why folks put so much stock in such things, anyway. What I mean is, how a feller talks has nothing to do with the way he shoots. Out here, it's best to shoot straight and leave the talking to others."

"It's important to come from a good family. Breeding and background are important," she maintained, still snipping away.

Judging by the pile of hair around me, I was pretty near scalped by now, and I was tempted to run a hand across my head. But from the way she ran those scissors, I was afraid I'd pull back a hand that was shy a couple of fingers.

I wasn't sure I agreed with all of what she said, but I kept my big mouth shut for a change. Afraid that we were heading for another fight, I asked her to tell me about the balls.

She took a minute to think about it before she replied. "You should see one. They are so grand, so monumental. The gleaming carriages with pretty women and handsome men inside. Of course, there is always music and dancing."

"Sounds like a box social," I commented, shifting my gun to a more comfortable position. She noticed the move-

ment and frowned. I got the impression
she didn't care for guns much.

"What is a box social? Tell me about
them."

"Pretty much what you said about
balls, 'cept that the carriages are usually
buckboards. Not all the women are pretty
or the men handsome," I explained.
"Maybe they ain't grand like your balls,
but they sure are fun."

"It's getting late," Laura said as she
put her scissors away. "I must help Kitty
with supper."

While we were walking up to the
house, Kitty came out to call us to supper. While Laura's attention was dis-
tracted, I ran my hand over my head.
Feeling what was left of my hair, I sure
hoped it didn't turn cold. My hat had a
few holes in it, and this haircut wasn't
made for a drafty hat.

I was surprised to see Chase pulled up
to the table. His face was drawn and pale,
but he was there.

"Mr. Chase, you should be in bed,"
Laura scolded him mildly.

"I never was one to lie in bed, ma'am,

and I guess I'm too old and set in my ways to change now," Chase told her.

Laura headed for a chair at the table. Now, I don't know much about manners, but I knew a man was supposed to hold a chair while a lady sat down. Quick as a wink, I stepped up to that chair and pulled it back for her.

"Why, thank you, Mr. Becker," Laura said, surprised.

To tell the truth, it made me feel good to do it for her. Her words and smile made me feel even better.

"You look very nice, Mr. Becker," Kitty said from the other side of the table.

My face burned, but I managed to mumble a thank-you.

"I heard you had a bath today," Chase commented with a sly smile.

I gave him a hard look, and he wiped that smile right off his face. "I'm planning on going for help tomorrow. Where would be the best place to go?" I asked, dishing myself some stew. I was watching Chase, but I saw the evil look that Laura threw my way. Now what did I do? Oh, yeah, I should've passed the stew around before horning in myself.

"There's a little town off to the west," Chase answered. He told me the best trail to take, and we figured that if I left two hours shy of daylight, I could be back late the same night.

"Go to the Last Chance Saloon," Chase said between mouthfuls of stew. "Bartender's name is Riley. Tell him I sent you. He'll pass the word. Owes me a favor, Riley does."

I figured on getting up early, so I pushed back from the table and headed for my bedroll. "Thanks for the supper, Miss Kitty. It sure was tasty," I said, stopping at the door. "And thanks for the haircut, ma'am."

Later on, rolling out my bedroll, I thought it over and decided to come back. I knew I'd never feel right with myself if I went off and deserted those two women. That clout on the head must've knocked the sense right out of me. Why, to think that I'd been scared of Laura!

Being a mite tired, I went right to sleep, but sometime in the night I awakened.

What woke me I wasn't sure. With as little movement as possible, I scanned the darkness. I could see nothing out of place, but it was almost pitch-dark. Straining my ears, I lay back and listened to the night.

Well, the first thing I knew, my mind was on that redheaded woman. It sure was nice the way we had talked this afternoon. Without warning, the thought came to me that she'd make someone a durned fine wife. This was a nice place to settle down and maybe have a whole raft of kids.

All of a sudden I gave a start. What was I doing—thinking of settling down, and marrying up with that redheaded woman? Huh! Witch-woman—that's what she was. Why, she must have put a spell on me to think such thoughts, and if I was going to make it up to Oregon, I'd best forget her. Yes sir, tomorrow I'd best take out and keep right on riding. But even as I thought that, I knew I wouldn't. It wasn't in me to leave them in the lurch.

Anyway, I had a floor to finish. And

maybe I'd stay and help Dickie build the house. Build it strong, to last, and big enough to hold a whole brood of kids.

With a groan, I realized I was doing it again, and I durned near crawled out of bed and shot myself. I wasn't ready to settle down, and even if I was, it wouldn't be with a sharp-tongued woman like that. Why, she would worry a man straight to the grave. He'd never know when she was going to stick her claws in him.

And all those rules she had, like saying "please" and "thank you." I just couldn't get used to all that.

As I thought of Laura, I drifted off to sleep. And I'd completely forgotten about the sounds that had woke me.

Chapter Six

The next morning I awoke early. Judging by the stars, it was about two hours before daylight. The night was quiet and foggy. Fog was unusual for this time of year, but we sure enough had some this morning, and the wisps lent an eerie quality that I didn't care for.

Moving quietly so as not to wake everyone in the house, I saddled my horse and started west for that town. It was cool, and despite the fog I was in a good mood this day. Soon I would have some help. I can tell you, watching over those two women sure did trouble a man. Not only did I have to worry about Ketchum's men gunning for me, but I had to watch those conniving women, and I had a sneaky suspicion that Chase was going to side with them against me. Oh, well, by this time tomorrow I'd be riding away from the ranch for good. But a little voice in my head told me this was not so.

I couldn't leave till I'd had a meeting with one Barry Ferriss. From what Garland Chase had told me, I figured that Ferriss would hunt me down if I tried to leave. If that was the case, I'd just as soon meet him on my own terms. I searched my mind to see if I was afraid to meet Ferriss, and found out that I was not. I realized that one of us would die if we met, and it could be me. Even though I knew this, I was not afraid. When the time came, I'd do what I had to do.

Chase had mentioned that Ferriss was a little crazy. He couldn't stand to have folks think that someone might beat him with a gun. That in itself was crazy as far as I was concerned. Me, I didn't want folks to think I was good with a gun. First thing you knew, some punk like Ferriss would decide to see if he was better. Since I had stood up to Chase, folks figured me for a dangerous man. Pretty soon, Ferriss would hear talk of it, and he'd have to show everyone he was the better man.

Yes sir, a reputation like that could get a man in a pile of trouble. Seemed like I always had enough trouble without inviting more.

The sun coming up made me feel better as the fog burned off. I should have been considering those sounds I had heard last night, and kept my guard up. Instead, I thought about Laura.

The sun warmed my shoulders and felt good this morning. There was no doubt that Laura was a beautiful young woman. One thing about it, she would keep a man on his toes. If he married her, life would never be dull. In fact, most times it might be more lively than a man could stand.

Why was I thinking of marriage? Oh, sure, I wanted a home someday, but I wanted to see more country. I couldn't deny that pleading call from the wild country.

My daydreams were shattered by the sharp bang of a shot, and I felt a hot lash across my shoulders. Instinctively, I rolled out of the saddle.

As soon as I hit the ground, I scooted behind a pile of rocks. Lucky thing I had been carrying my rifle, because without it, I would have been at the mercy of that dry-gulcher. Well, maybe it hadn't been all luck. I'd had a feeling this morning that I might need that rifle.

Lying behind those rocks, I tried to calculate where he might be holed up. Probably up on the slope and slightly behind me. He had let me pass by him, then took his shot.

Another shot broke the silence. I ducked, then realized that the shot had come nowhere near me.

As the echoes of the shot died away, I heard my roan scream in pain. Peeking around the rock, I saw him take a few steps, then collapse in a heap. Cursing bitterly, I hugged the ground in my tiny hollow of rocks.

A lump came to my throat when I thought about losing that roan. As I wiped my sleeve across my eyes, I heard the rider leave. Now what the heck was that all about? Did my attacker think he had killed me? I didn't think so, but I could see no other reason for him to leave.

My sadness at the loss of the roan left me and was replaced by red-hot anger. I was going to get that man if I had to chase him on foot plumb back to town.

I started to get up when a bullet smacked into a rock right beside me. Startled, I fell back down and hugged the ground. There must be two of them. No sooner did I think that than another thought hit home.

That other rider was going to fetch Ketchum and the crew. They would raid the ranch! Desperately, I searched for a way out of this hole. It boiled down to the fact that I was going to have to kill that man up yonder. From his last shot, I had a rough idea where he would be, but the knowledge did little to cheer me. He was a long way off and he had come mighty close with that snap shot.

A cold fear crept up my spine. If Ketchum's men attacked the ranch while the women were outside, they would be helpless to stop them. As much as I feared for my friends, I reminded myself to be extra careful.

If I was going to get myself out of this

mess, I'd have to use my head. Control-
ling my impatience, I took another look
at the situation. My attacker could not
see me—of that I was sure. If he *could*
see me, I would already be dead. He
might be working in close for a shot. I
dearly wanted to look around, but
chances were that if I raised my head, he
would shoot it off.

The way things stood, he could walk
right down on me and there wasn't a
thing I could do to stop him. I couldn't
risk rising up for a look. Sooner or later
he was going to slip down on me.

The thing I had to do was move. The
best way looked off to the left, where
some rocks offered cover. Only problem
was I'd be exposed for a second while I
moved from rock to rock, and a second
was all that gent would need to put a bullet in my brisket.

Glancing off to the right, I felt discour-
aged. There just wasn't much cover to be
had down thataway. Then I spied a little
scrubby mesquite bush just beyond the
edge of the hollow.

Now that little ole bush wasn't going

to stop a bullet, but it would offer some concealment. Besides, I had a feeling that whoever was up yonder would be concentrating on the other side.

Although risky, I felt the time had come to take a chance. Slowly, I inched my way out of the hollow and behind the bush. Any second now I expected to hear a shot and feel bullets tearing through me. Fear tensed my muscles till they ached, but I forced myself to move slow and steady.

Once behind the bush, I took a deep breath, feeling reasonably safe. If that feller hadn't seen me by now, chances were that he wouldn't. Even though I didn't have the protection of the rocks, my position was much better. At least now I could see.

I considered just waiting till he decided to show himself, but he might not do that. He might be content with simply keeping me pinned down until the attack on the ranch was over. So like it or not, I was going to have to get him.

While I watched, the roan jumped up and took off. I could see blood on his side as he galloped away, and I raised my rifle to finish him off, but I couldn't see through the sights for the mist in my eyes. By the time it cleared, the roan was out of sight.

I figured that that horse was going off someplace to die. I hated to see him suffer, but I couldn't help that now.

Hoping to find something I'd missed earlier, I took a long look around. Getting out of here wasn't going to be easy. The slope in front of me rolled away long and gentle. What's more, it was smooth and pretty much free of anything to hide behind. Behind me, the ground fell away for about ten yards and then sort of leveled out. I contemplated charging up the hill. The only thing was, I knew I'd never make it. It looked like I was trapped.

Would they be alert at the ranch? If Garland Chase was awake, they would be, because he feared an attack as much as I did. I'd have to trust him to have someone on watch. How good a watch would the two women keep?

A sick feeling slowly settled in the pit of my stomach. Looking about, I searched wildly for a means of escaping, but try as I might, I couldn't see anything to do. In the back of my mind I knew that each passing second brought Ketchum's men closer to the ranch.

Chapter Seven

Right about then, I was feeling down in the dumps. Here I was, hugging the ground, fearing for my life while Laura needed me.

Even though she was raking me over the coals most of the time I had known her, I had grown very fond of that woman. I would miss her cooking when I rode off. I'd never admit it to her, but she was a durned good cook.

There was something else about her that stuck in my mind. She was always showing me up, but there was a directness about her that I liked. She had a way of looking right at a body and speaking her mind.

The sound of a boot rubbing against rock shook me out of my thoughts. Jerking my head around, I saw Murdock standing at the edge of the hollow I'd just left, his rifle pointed into the hollow.

Just as I saw him, his eyes came up and rested right on me. Without thinking, I rolled onto my back and drew my pistol. His rifle swung to cover me as I fired. My shot spun him around and he lost his rifle. Teeth bared in a fierce growl, he dropped his hand for his six-gun.

My first shot had hit him in the left shoulder, but it didn't slow him any. As he clawed for his gun, I fired twice.

He went down, but he wasn't dead. And he wasn't through yet! Struggling to sit, he raised his pistol as if it weighed a ton. Jumping to my feet, I tried to cover the distance between us before he got his gun up. I lashed out with my foot and kicked the gun from his hand. The force of the kick knocked him back in the sand.

"Got careless. Always knew it would happen someday," he said hoarsely.

As I looked down at him, I knew it was only a matter of minutes before he would be dead. Those .45 slugs had torn great holes in his chest. It was a wonder he was still breathing.

"Just wanted you to know that I had nothing to do with shooting your horse," Murdock said with a cough. "It was that stupid Wes. He's the one that shot your horse. I almost shot him for that myself. I never should've let Dutch talk me into bringing him along. He's been nothing but trouble." A fit of coughing shook his entire body, leaving him paler than you could believe. "If I'd been alone, I would have waited for a better shot, but that Wes was so danged impatient."

He was dying, and I felt sorry for him. In my book, he had got just what he deserved, but still, I hated to leave him to die alone.

He was so quiet for a while that I thought he had died. Then I heard a weak chuckle. "You durned near gave us the slip this morning. Ole Wes, he could sleep through a tornado, and I almost missed hearing you." He gave another low chuckle. "Now I wish I had. You go on and help them girls. Ain't nothing you can do for me," he finished.

What he said was true, but I felt reluctant to leave. "I'll come back and give you a decent burial," I said finally.

He gave a faint nod. "My horse is up yonder. Take him if you've a mind to."

"Thanks," I said. Then I picked up my rifle and trudged up the hill.

It took me only a few minutes to locate his horse. For just a second, I stared at the bloody trail of the roan. I wanted to follow it and put that horse out of his misery, but the trail led away from the ranch and I couldn't spare the time. I jumped into the saddle and, slapping spurs to that nag, took off like the wind.

Right then, I made myself a promise. I'd find the gent that shot my horse and we'd have a serious chat. Wes was the feller with Chase that morning. I would remember him.

It was quite a ways back to the ranch, so I slowed the horse to a fast trot. I just hoped that Garland Chase was alert.

Although I rode like all of creation was chasing me, soon I'd have to give my horse a rest. Cursing, I wished that I had that ole roan horse. Ugly he may have been, but that horse was fast, and he could hold a pace that would kill most horses.

Thinking of that horse suffering by himself made me mad clear through. He was mean and ornery, but he didn't deserve to suffer and die like this. As soon as I made sure the ranch was safe, I would come back and do everything I could for the roan. And afterward, I'd go hunting for a man.

I stopped Murdock's horse, stepped down, and from the canteen hung on the saddle poured my hat full and gave that horse a good drink. I took a long pull from the canteen, hung it back on the saddle, and began to walk.

Walking was something that I never cared for, and doing it did nothing to help my temperament. Slowly, I worked myself into quite a rage. Right about then I felt ready to take on Ketchum and his whole crew. I'd never been one to sit back and think. Like I said, my way was to bull in and let the chips fall where they would.

After walking a couple of miles, I stopped for a brief rest. With my bandanna, I mopped the sweat from my face and neck. Sweat trickled into the scratch across the back of my shoulders, and it stung something fierce. After giving the horse another drink, I spoke a few words of encouragement. Horses always respond if you treat them right and talk to them. Then I swung back into the saddle and started off.

Everything appeared to be quiet when I spotted the ranch, but never one to trust appearances, I left the horse in a grove of trees and began to work my way closer. Moving slow and careful, I eased down that long slope behind the house. About forty yards from the house, I slid in behind a clump of cactus and decided to stay put.

Either the fighting was already over or it hadn't started yet. Whichever, the best thing for me was to stay put.

The thing that troubled me was the lack of movement. Normally, Laura or Kitty would be working outside by now. Of course, if Chase feared an attack, he'd probably keep everyone inside. Even as I told myself that, a part of me still thought that Ketchum's men had already been here. While I hid on this slope, the McCrays could already be dead in their house, or maybe dragged off as captives.

For the hundredth time, I told myself that the best thing to do was wait. It would do the McCrays no good if I got myself killed. If any of Ketchum's men were behind the house, they'd see me if I made a charge for it. Not only would they see me, but they'd have me dead in their sights.

Raising my head a mite, I scanned the slope around me. I could see no one, but that did little to cheer me. The slope was littered with stones and cut with small gullies. If Ketchum's men were hiding on the slope, as I was, they'd be hard to spot. As long as they didn't move, seeing them would be danged near impossible.

I'd just about decided that Ketchum's men weren't about when I heard his voice. "There's no need for any more kill-ing," he said.

So there *had* been a fight! Evidently the McCrays had held them off, and now Ketchum was ready to talk.

"I'll give you ten thousand dollars for the place," Ketchum shouted.

Wow! That was a lot of money. 'Course, I didn't believe for a second that Ketchum intended to pay. His offer was just an excuse to get the McCrays out of the house.

Nobody answered from the house. That must have angered Ketchum, because shots rang out from around front. Almost in front of me, I saw two men rise from the ground and move toward the house.

Why wasn't someone watching the rear? Were the McCrays dead? If they weren't, why wasn't somebody stopping these two?

I hated to shoot without warning, and though this here was war, I took aim just past the ear of one of them and squeezed off my shot. When he didn't take my hint and leave, I finished him off and then shifted my aim to the other one. He was close enough for me to see the surprise and viciousness on his face as he turned. I held my aim for just a second, and then I fired again.

I was so intent on the two men in front of me that I missed seeing the rifle being poked out the back window. I just got to my feet when somebody took a shot at me from the house. Surprised, I let out a mighty roar and dropped flat again. I heard a startled cry from inside, and the rifle was withdrawn. As the gun disappeared back through the window, I was up and running. Running past the two dead men, I made a beeline for that side door.

Bullets whined all around me, so I didn't take the time to open the door. Now, I've worked hard all my life, and as a result, I'm an uncommonly strong man. When I put my shoulder into that door with a full head of steam behind me, well, that latch broke with a screech and the door swung open and bounced off the wall.

I was almost in the middle of the room before I could stop. And the greeting I got wasn't quite what I'd been expecting. Chase was slumped against the wall, obviously unconscious. The McCrays were gathered around him, staring at me with blank looks. Then I noticed what I'd overlooked—one of Ketchum's men leaned against the table.

I didn't recognize him, but that wasn't important. The main thing was that he had his gun out, and it was pointed right in my direction.

"Well, now, ain't this nice?" he said with a smile, and I could see his broken yellow teeth. "All of you right here together. The boss will be pleased."

The shooting outside had stopped, and that worried me some more. In a matter of minutes they'd be crashing through the front door and I'd have the whole bunch to deal with. When I'd told myself earlier that I wanted to take the whole bunch on, I'd only been kidding.

Taking a step back to put the women more out of the line of fire, I tensed to make a play. Trouble was, my rifle was angled toward the floor and his ole six was pointed right at my belly. I'd heard tell of people who'd beaten the drop, but I wasn't sure that I could. Still, I had to try.

"Empty your hands, mister," he ordered.

Alert for anything to give me an edge, I let my rifle clatter to the floor. Then, out of the corner of my eye, I saw my chance. Garland Chase was drawing a pistol from underneath his shirt. He was doing it painfully slow, but nonetheless that gun was coming out.

That hombre must've seen it too, because his eyes darted that way and he shifted his aim. The second his eyes left me, my hand swooped for my pistol. Sure enough, he saw me, but for just a second he was undecided about what to do.

Deciding that I was the bigger threat, he swung his gun back toward me. But he was too late. I'd already hauled out my gun and let 'er pop. The bullet plugged him dead center, and as he fell back on top of it, the table broke under his weight. I let out a groan, because Laura would raise hob over that.

Scooping up my rifle, I ran to the window. Sure enough, Ketchum's men were right on top of us. Almost by itself, my rifle came up and centered on the chest of a big fat man with a red beard.

Ketchum's men saw my rifle barrel poking out the window, and, screeching to a halt, they tried to scramble for cover. It didn't help the fat one, though. Before he could stop, I nailed him. That bullet seemed to let the air out of him as he sort of just melted to the ground. As fast as I could, I emptied the rifle at the fleeing men. Howls of pain told me that some of my bullets had scored.

All of a sudden I was caught up in the battle. What I mean is, I snatched up another rifle, Chase's, I suppose. Jacking a shell into the chamber, I busted out the front door and chased after them. Firing as I ran, I made only about five or six yards before the rifle ran dry.

Just about then, some of my good sense returned and I realized I was standing in the wide-open yard. Now it was my turn to scurry for cover, and with two long steps I dived behind the water trough. I wouldn't have made it, but somebody opened up from inside the house.

When I looked back at it, I caught a

fleeting glimpse of Dickie's face, and I reminded myself to thank that boy, for he'd sure enough saved my bacon.

Lying behind the water trough, I was more than a little shaken. What in Sam Hill had come over me anyway? It was a wonder I hadn't been killed. I'd been pretty cool until I had seen that frightened look on Laura's face. Then a blinding rage had gripped me and filled me with a desire to lash out at what frightened her.

I tried to control my breathing as I plugged fresh shells into that Winchester. Good sense told me to stay put. That water trough was made of oak, so I was safe as long as I kept down. Thing was, we'd caught them flat-footed, and since we had them backing up, I had the feeling that now was the time to keep pushing.

I was sure that some of Ketchum's men were in the barn, but how many? Not more than two, I'd bet, and if I was going to make some moves, that would be the place to start. 'Course, if there were more men in the barn than I had figured. . . .

I didn't bother to answer myself on that one.

Rolling onto my back, I reloaded my pistol and shoved it into the holster. Then I clutched my rifle and looked to the sky. Now, I'm not what you would call a praying man, but right then I was sure hoping and asking for some kind of help.

Next, I sprang to my feet and as quick as a wink I took four long steps and lunged inside the barn.

Three men were holding a heated discussion in the center of the barn when I burst in on them. One held a rifle, and I knew I'd have to handle him first.

Running full speed, I tilted my rifle, holding it one-handed like a pistol, and I drove a shot at the man. Without missing a step, I slashed out with the barrel and hit one of them in the head with a solid thump. As he fell, he bumped into his companion and spoiled his shot.

That gave me just enough time to flop over the partition and into a stall. I had recognized the other feller out there. He was wearing a checked shirt, just like the one I'd seen back yonder. I figured him for the skunk who'd shot my horse.

"You shot my horse. I ought to kill you for that," I said conversationally.

Wes didn't answer, but I knew he was out there. Laying my rifle aside, I drew my pistol and dived headlong out of the stall. I fell on my shoulder and rolled over. My head spun slightly as I located Wes. We shot at the same time and we both missed.

Wes didn't have the kind of courage to stand and swap shots, so he broke for the door instead. I snapped a quick shot at him and missed again. He should have remembered the folks in the house, because as soon as he ran out of the barn, a shot sounded.

The bullet stopped him and spun him around toward me. He was trapped and he knew it, but he sneered as he aimed his gun at me. I could feel no pity for the man who shot my horse, so I steadied my pistol and fired. He grunted. Dust jumped from his shirt as the bullet struck. For a moment he swayed in the yard on rubbery legs, and then he lay sprawled on the ground.

It had grown deathly quiet. The only sound was that of my own ragged breathing. Had Ketchum's men pulled out or were they creeping up behind the barn?

All of a sudden I didn't care for this barn, a poor place to try to defend. The only openings were the two big doors on either end. The front didn't worry me much, for the McCrays could cover that from the house. The back on the other hand was wide-open. If Ketchum's men rushed me from there, I wouldn't be able to stop them.

After retrieving my rifle, I went to the back door, where I took a chance and poked my head out. No shot sounded, and no one was in sight. I stepped back and took a minute to contemplate. It appeared Ketchum had pulled off. I couldn't be sure, though, so I decided to wait. No sense in getting shot just because I was impatient.

Twenty minutes passed and nothing happened, so I took another peek. Since nothing was in sight, I decided to go look.

I wished for a pair of moccasins. My last pair had worn out, and sometime soon I'd have to pay an Indian woman to make me another pair. Briefly, I wondered if Laura could make moccasins. Wasn't likely, her being from the city. I could make a pair myself, but I hated doing so.

Quietly, I eased out into the bushes and worked my way around to where I figured their horses would be. I found no horses but plenty of tracks. It certainly looked like they had pulled out, but I'm a cautious sort of man and I circled the ranch just to be sure. Only thing I found was a few scattered drops of blood. We'd banged them up some—that was certain.

As I walked through the barn on my way to the house, I noticed that the man I'd walloped on the head with my rifle was gone. It was just as well, because I didn't want any prisoners.

When I went down to the cabin, the McCrays' faces were as drawn and pale as could be. Garland Chase was conscious, but he had a pale, sick look on his face. "Are they gone?" Kitty asked.

"They had enough for today," I told her.

"But they'll be back, won't they?" Laura asked.

"They'll be back. It ain't over as long as Ketchum is still alive."

"Or Barry Ferriss," Chase said weakly. "He's a paid killer and loves his work. Sure am glad to see you. I was just about played out."

I helped him to his feet and into the bedroom. Every movement brought him pain. I'd been shot before and knew what he was feeling. Even the smallest movement stretches the skin around the wound.

Once he was in bed, I checked his wounds. Even though they had broken open and bled some, they looked to be healing. He began resting easily, so I left and went to the kitchen.

Dickie waited for me, his face flushed with excitement. He seemed to be recovering from the fight remarkably well. Seeing him made me feel old and tired, and I plopped down into a chair.

"I figured out why Ketchum wants to kill us," Dickie said excitedly.

"What's that?" I asked.

Before Dickie could answer, Laura placed some thick sandwiches in front of us. "You must be hungry," she said, touching her hair self-consciously.

"Thank you, ma'am," I said, surprised at her attitude. She had never struck me as being shy before. I didn't have long to wonder about her attitude. Dickie was about to bust with his news about Ketchum.

Chapter Eight

Drawing back a chair, Dickie sat down across from me and said, "I saw Ketchum today."

Well, that wasn't nearly as interesting as those sandwiches. After all, I'd seen Ketchum too. I took a sandwich from the platter and then pushed it across the table at Dickie.

"Ketchum's real name is Dutch Blackburn, and I saw him murder a man in St. Louis," he said, ignoring the food. "It isn't the ranch he wants. He just wants us out of here."

Now things made sense. But, unfortunately, I now also knew Ketchum would never give up this fight. He had too much to lose.

As soon as I'd finished my sandwich, I turned Murdock's horse loose in the corral and threw my saddle on Dickie's horse. I rode out of the yard with a heavy heart. That horse of mine lay out there somewhere, perhaps suffering. While I rode, my earlier anger settled into a deep rage. That Ketchum was getting under my skin. It was high time that somebody did something about him.

After a few miles I spotted a dust cloud. In my present state of mind, I threw caution to the wind and touched a spur to Dickie's horse. Shortly, I saw my roan horse shuffling down the trail toward the McCray ranch.

He was limping badly, almost dragging his right foreleg. For a brief second, a smile of joy lit my face as I watched the roan. Then the smile faded as I realized what I might have to do. I ran my fingers along the butt of my gun. For once, the feel of the pistol gave me no comfort.

As I dismounted, that horse nuzzled my chest and for once didn't try to nip me with his teeth. Holding that horse around the neck, I drew my pistol, closed my eyes, and placed the gun to his head. I held it there for a long time, but couldn't squeeze the trigger.

I holstered the pistol and bent to look at the wound, which didn't look so bad. The bullet went in behind the right shoulder and came out the front. If no bones were broken, it might heal. The problem was keeping him off his feet long enough for the wound to heal.

Looking the wound over very carefully, I decided that no bones were broken.

Taking a chance, I led the roan back to the ranch. It proved to be a heartbreaking task, because the roan limped every step of the way. I could see the pain in his eyes, and several times I almost stopped and put him out of his misery.

Finally, we made it to the ranch and I led him into the barn. After locking him in a stall, I set about cleansing the wound. There wasn't any way to put on a bandage, so I left it open. I stayed with him a long time, talking to him and trying to keep him calm.

While I petted the roan, a slow anger came over me. Usually, I fought these angers, but this time I didn't even try. Ketchum had to pay. Till now, he'd had it too easy, but I was fixing to change that.

Come nightfall, I was going to slip over to his place. I didn't know how effective a one-man attack would be, but I figured to worry them a bit. Leaving the roan to rest, I trudged back up to the house. I felt tired to the bone, but tired or not, I had a few things to do. First I wanted to have a talk with Garland Chase. I needed to get an idea of the layout of Ketchum's ranch.

Chase was sitting on the porch, and I dragged up a bench and sat down beside him. "I been thinking about slipping over to Ketchum's place tonight," I told him.

"Sounds good. I'll go with you," Chase offered.

I looked at him in amazement. He could barely walk across the porch, but one look was all I needed to tell he was dead serious. "Maybe it would be better for you to stay here," I said. "I might have to get out of there pretty fast." I liked Chase and didn't want to offend him. "I'd feel better with you here while I'm gone." Which was true enough.

Chase laughed. "Okay, I'll stay behind, but don't low-rate Dickie. He hung right in there during the whole fight. Fact is, I thought he was going to kill me."

"How'd that come about?"

"While we waited for Dutch's boys to work up the guts to attack, I sent the women to watch the back. Ole Dutch, he ain't the smartest guy in the world, and he sent a couple of fellers round back. He figured that when they opened up back there, we'd all rush to the rear of the house and then they could storm the front."

Chase paused to reload his lungs and look around. "Dickie wanted to help his sisters, but I told him to stay put. He must've thought I was still working for Dutch, 'cause he turned his rifle on me and was ready to pull the trigger. It was a good thing Ketchum's boys came fogging it up to the front about then."

I laughed at the thought of it. "Aw, that's nothing," I told him. "One of them gals did take a shot at me!"

"Sorry about that," Kitty said from the door, "but you jumped up waving that rifle. How was I supposed to know you weren't one of them?"

I thought about telling her she could have tried looking, but she'd already shot at me once today. Considering that, I figured I'd best keep my smart remarks to myself. While we talked, Dickie and Laura came outside and sat down.

"What I can't figure out is why Ketchum is so worried about us," Laura told us. "I mean, he's killed several people since we've been here."

"Now there's a question," Chase said to Dickie. "I've been thinking about that. Did you know the man he killed?"

"No, I never saw him before," Dickie replied with a shrug.

"Whoever this guy was, he must have had some friends, because he sure has got Dutch scared," Chase said thoughtfully.

We talked awhile longer, then I remembered that I had a promise to keep. "I've got something to do," I said.

"Do you need some help?" Dickie asked.

"No, you stay here in case Ketchum comes back." I really didn't think

Ketchum would be back, but you can never tell.

"What do you have to do that's so important?" Laura wanted to know.

"I've got to bury a man. I gave my word," I said simply.

"Murdock?" Chase asked, and I nodded. "I was afraid for you. I got to thinking that I forgot to warn you about him."

"He made his try, and I'll tell you he came close to stretching my hide."

"First time I ever heard of Murdock missing," Chase said, rubbing his chin thoughtfully. "But don't let up. There's plenty of men in Ketchum's crew that would shoot you in the back if they got the chance."

Chapter Nine

Just after dark, I slipped down to the corral. Taking a moment, I looked in on that roan horse of mine. He raised his head to look at me but didn't get up. I gave him a pat and then threw my saddle on one of Dickie's horses. I had a feeling that Ketchum's men would be tired and maybe sleeping soundly. Anyway, I was going over to pay them my respects.

The cool night air soothed my tired muscles. I was always one to enjoy the night. The world seemed so peaceful after folks quit their fussin' and feudin' and went to bed.

Relaxing in the saddle, I let the horse pick his way along. I wasn't in any particular hurry and wanted to give Ketchum's men time to get bedded down. I noticed all the movement of the night. I saw an old owl swooping down on an unsuspecting mouse, and a coyote darting from me. I glimpsed a fleeting shadow at the edge of the trail, and my hand fell to the butt of my pistol.

"Hold on there, young feller. I mean you no harm," a gravelly voice called out.

"What do you want?" I kept my hand on my gun while I waited for his answer.

"You're Dan Becker, ain't you?"

"That's right," I answered coolly. "I'd appreciate it if you would come out where I can see you."

I heard a dry laugh. Then he stepped out carefully on the trail. He was a dried-up old man who looked old enough to have been on the Mayflower. Even in the poor light I could see the sour expression on his wrinkled face.

"I was just heading out to the McCray place to have a word with you. A couple of fellers came into town on the stage today," he said, watching me like a hawk.

"Should that mean anything to me?"

The old man shrugged his thin shoulders. "Maybe, maybe not. They was dudes from St. Louie. The big one, Clayton Owen Davis, allowed that he was fixin' to marry Laura McCray."

All of a sudden I felt like I had been kicked in the gut by a mule. My breath got trapped in my lungs and I couldn't talk for a minute. "What are you telling me that for?" I asked finally.

"I heard you was sweet on that Laura gal. I thought if you wanted, I'd take care of them two fellas for you."

"Why do you think I'm sweet on her?" I demanded, my tone sounding rough.

The old man chuckled but he didn't smile. I got the impression that he didn't smile very often. "Well, you've been staying out there, helping them out. Folks in town figured you and her were gonna get hitched."

"I'm just helping them out. We ain't getting married!" I declared loudly.

The old man laughed again, and this time I thought I could see a ghost of a smile on his lips. But in the pale moonlight I couldn't be sure. "Whatever you say. But like I said, I can get a couple of the boys around town to whup the tar out of them two and throw them on the first stage out of town."

"Why do you want to help me?" I asked.

"I liked the way you bucked up to Ketchum and his boys. Old Dutch never bothered me any, but I don't hold with everything he done, either. Besides, you helped some kin of mine one time. You recall a boy you pulled out of a fight down in El Paso?"

I did remember. I'd been playing poker when this kid sat down at the table. It soon became clear that this kid didn't know anything about poker. He was pulling stunts like drawing three cards to fill a straight. The problem was, he was drawing the cards he needed.

The kid was having one of those nights when the cards fell his way. If I hadn't known better, I'd swear he was cheating, but I'd been watching him mighty close.

The boy had won a couple of hundred bucks when some of the guys at the table decided that he had cheated. And they also decided to string him up on the nearest tree. That's when I stuck my big nose into things, and since I had my ole pistol out and the hammer eared back, they decided to take their losing in a more graceful manner.

"That boy was my sister's kid," the old man went on. "So if you want me to do something about them two dudes, I'd be happy to oblige."

I was sorely tempted to take him up on his offer, but I knew I'd never feel right afterward. "No. Just bring them out to the ranch in the morning," I said heavily.

"Suit yourself," he said with a shrug. "But they might get themselves beat up. That Clayton, he's been thumbing his nose at the whole town, and folks are mighty sore."

"See if you can keep them out of trouble till morning," I said.

"If it was me, I'd send them packing," the old man grumbled, backing off the trail.

I heard the creak of leather as he mounted. For a long time I listened to the fading sounds as he rode back to town. Feeling old and as tired as death, I touched a spur to Dickie's horse.

Pretty soon I came upon a creek with a good-sized stream running through it. Unless I was mistaken, this was Snake Creek, named for the way it meandered along. From what Garland Chase had told me, I knew that this creek met up with Cord Creek, and that Ketchum's ranch was set right in the fork where the two streams met.

I was getting close, so I stepped down and tied my bandanna over my horse's nostrils because I didn't want him to whinny and give me away. I'd be coming up downwind of the ranch, so there was no danger of Ketchum's horses smelling me.

Weaving through the trees, I finally caught a glimpse of Ketchum's spread, and I gave a low whistle. It was one heck of a nice place. Tree-lined streams ringed three sides, and the fourth side was an open valley with knee-deep grass. The house, barn, and bunkhouse formed a triangle with a corral filled with horses attached to the barn.

I was well back in the trees, and before moving closer, I scrutinized the place.

The one guard on duty was relaxing in a rocker in front of the bunkhouse.

I tied my horse and worked closer. When I reached the edge of the trees, I had a decision to make. I couldn't cross the fifty yards of open grass without being seen, but I could circle around and come up behind the bunkhouse. Problem was, I couldn't do that and keep my eyes on the guard. On the other hand, I could wait and hope he made a turn around the buildings.

It was still a bit shy of midnight. I made up my mind to wait, and I settled against a tree where I could watch the man on guard. I was well back in the trees, so I wasn't worried about him seeing me. I'd be just another dark shadow.

For the next twenty minutes a battle raged to see who was going to fall asleep first, him or me. It had been a long day for me, and I was feeling it. Being this tired worried me, because my reflexes wouldn't be as sharp. But worried or not, I stuck right in there. Stubbornness, a quality I'd had my life long, wouldn't let me quit. Guess I wasn't as smart as some.

I just didn't have the sense to quit sometimes.

As my eyelids drooped, the guard rose
from his chair and stretched. I waited.
The guard rubbed his eyes and looked
around. Then he circled the yard.

As soon as he walked behind the big
house, I would run for the barn. The big
door in the front stood open and inviting.
Still watching the guard, I inched out of
my hiding place, and the second he
rounded the corner of the house, I was
off and running.

Once inside, I was forced to slow up,
as the floor was littered with tools. A
small door in the rear was open to allow
in the breeze. A little bit of the moonlight
filtered in through the two doors, but the
inside was still barely visible. Carefully,
I worked my way to the rear of the barn
and crouched by the door.

Listening intently, I waited for the
guard to come by. In a matter of seconds
I heard his footsteps and saw the shad-
owy outline of his back. In one swift step,
I was outside and right behind him.

"Make one peep and I'll blow a hole

plumb through you," I snarled, ramming my pistol in the small of his back. "Now back inside."

Using some old bridles, I tied and gagged him. Then I took a chance and lit a match and took a look around. In one stall I saw something that really pleased me—a keg of blasting powder. Beside the powder leaned a sack of nails, and when I saw them, a plan began to form in my head.

What I needed now was some rope. It took only a minute to find the crew's saddles, and sure enough each one had a rope on it. Chuckling to myself, I drew my knife and cut the cinch on every saddle. Knowing gun hands like I did, I was sure this would upset them more than anything. These men were gun hands because it was easier than working, and they wouldn't like having to repair their saddles.

Taking their ropes, I tiptoed down to the bunkhouse. After tying several ropes together, I strung them across the door of the bunkhouse. Then I hustled back to the barn for the nails and the blasting powder. The nails I scattered on the ground in front of the bunkhouse door. I even took the time to poke a few in the ground so that the sharp ends were pointing up. While I made my preparations, I chuckled with anticipation. Once I was finished, I stood back to look at what I had done. That's when I saw the empty whiskey bottles against the bunkhouse. These I lined up in the midst of my nails.

Next, I scooped up the powder keg and took it behind the barn. With my knife, I punched a hole in the top of the keg and strung out a line of powder from the barn to the rear wall of the bunkhouse. Against the wall, I made a small pile of powder and placed the keg right in the center of it.

My tiredness forgotten, I ran to where my horse was tied and brought him up behind the barn. After tying the horse, I went to the line of powder. For a minute I rehearsed my plan, then took a match from my pocket and placed it between my teeth. Grinning around the match, I took up my rifle and busted the bottles I had placed in front of the door.

Almost instantly, Ketchum's men came pouring out of the bunkhouse. Most of them had on only their underwear, but all were armed, not that it did them much good, for as they charged out of the bunkhouse, my rope did just what I had hoped it would.

It was a pretty sight to see those would-be toughs rolling on the ground amidst the broken glass and nails. Their howls of pain were sweet music to me.

Just to add to their confusion, I fired a few shots among them. I wasn't trying to hit any of them, just creating some confusion.

Howling and yelping, Ketchum's men dived back to the safety of their bunkhouse, with bullets from my rifle helping them along.

The shots still rang in my ears as I lit the match and dropped it into the trail of powder. Immediately, a low row of flames started for the bunkhouse.

I raced to my horse and swung into the saddle. No sooner was I aboard than a huge explosion rocked the air. For a while, the reins jerked angrily as I fought

to control my bucking horse. When I re-
gained control of him, I rode round the
barn and into the yard.

Once again, I was rewarded with the
sight of Ketchum's men scrambling outside. Some had dressed, but most had not.
The rope had done its job again, as many
of them were scrambling on the ground.

After slipping the empty rifle into the
scabbard, I became aware that the horses
in the corral were bucking and milling
around. Evidently, some splinters from
the explosion had struck them. The corral, a rawhide one, collapsed, and the way
those horses went streaming off into the
dark, you'd have thought their tails were
on fire.

All of this I caught out of the corner
of my eye. Most of my attention was on
the cursing men in the yard. Some of their
clothes smoldered, and a tiny flame
blazed in the corner of the bunkhouse.

A big, bearded man came out carrying
a rifle. He was paying no mind to the broken glass and nails under his bare feet,
nor was he bothered by the fact that his

underwear was smoking. His eyes searched the darkness for the culprit.

In one easy motion I flipped out my six-gun and fired as it came level. A big man, he was madder than a cat with a mashed tail, but when that bullet hit the ground right in front of his bare feet, he dived for the cover of the smoking bunkhouse.

I had a feeling that I'd just about worn out my welcome here, and that it was time to leave. Then, without warning, a shot rang out and a bullet struck the barn right behind my head. Whirling my horse, I saw Ketchum standing in the door of the big house. My quick turn had caused him to miss his second shot, and I was in no mood to give him another.

While spurring my horse, I snapped a quick shot at him. It must have missed, because he dived back inside. As I swept past the house, I sent a few bullets crashing through the windows, and then I rode the heck out of there.

Safely away, I pulled up the horse and reloaded my guns.

Thinking back on what I'd done, I was

pleased. Not that I'd done them any real damage, but it had been fun. Then I turned the horse toward the McCray ranch and started home.

Chapter Ten

Dawn broke as I came into sight of the Mc-Cray ranch. Smoke rose lazily from the chimney. Looking the place over from this angle, I had to admit that it held a certain beauty.

It was the type of terrain commonly found in the Southwest—a stream, surrounded by cottonwoods, running through a canyon. While most of the surrounding country was brown and dusty, the canyon was green.

I touched a spur to Dickie's horse and angled for the barn. Though dog-tired and hungry, I'd always been taught to care for my horse first, and the first thing I did was check on the roan. That horse of mine had a sick look in his eyes, but the wound looked okay. Both holes had scabbed over nicely, and as long as the fool critter didn't rub the scabs off, I figured he'd be fine. Right now, he was lying down and didn't look like he wanted to move.

After offering the roan a few words of encouragement, I stripped the saddle off Dickie's horse. I didn't figure we would have any trouble this morning, so I turned the rest of the horses out to graze.

For a minute, as I watched the critters, I tried to decide whether I was more tired or hungry. Finally hunger won out, and I trudged up to the house.

Laura ran halfway down to the barn to meet me. Realizing that she'd been worried, I got a warm feeling. It had been a long time since anyone had worried over me.

"Come in, Dan. Breakfast is ready," she said, taking me by the arm.

Garland Chase lingered at the table, sipping his coffee. He gave us a funny look and a knowing smile.

I felt uncomfortable standing there with a silly look on my face. Seemed like at times like this, I could never think of anything to say. Mad at myself and at Chase, I slouched into a chair.

While Laura went to dish up my breakfast, Kitty and Dickie rushed in from the garden. They both seemed real anxious to hear what I'd been up to. Before I could tell them, Chase cut me off and said, "It'll have to keep. We got company coming."

Sure enough, I could hear the sound of approaching horses, and I got out of my chair. I hadn't expected those dudes to get here so early. Why, they must have left about sunup. I gathered up my rifle and followed Chase out onto the porch. From over my shoulder, I told the McCrays to fetch their rifles and stand by the windows, just in case.

As I tipped my rifle over my shoulder, I leaned against one of the poles that supported the awning. Chase didn't have his rifle, but he was wearing his six-guns and was waiting just as I was. I wasn't sure if he was in shape for a fight, being wounded and all, but he looked ready. Men like Chase are born with a toughness, and it takes a lot to keep them down.

Something had been bothering me about the sound of the horses, and when they pulled into sight, I saw what it was.

It wasn't riders but a buckboard. They were still too far away for me to make out the occupants, but they appeared to be three or four men.

With a puzzled look on his face, Chase stared intently at the wagon. Like me, he was wary of a trap. I had a good idea who was in the wagon, but I kept my ideas to myself. "Looks harmless enough," I commented, trying to sound casual.

Chase shot me a hard look, but he didn't say anything until the buckboard pulled into the yard.

"What brings you out this way, Arky?" Chase asked as the buckboard pulled to a halt in front of us.

Meanwhile I surveyed the passengers, who appeared harmless. Two of them were dudes obviously, while the third was a leather-skinned old man, the same man I had spoken with last night. His face might be wrinkled, but his eyes were clear and sharp.

"Brought some visitors out to see the McCrays," he said, answering Chase's question. "This is Clayton Owen Davis and Malcolm Judson." He turned a pair of cold, gray eyes on me. "How you doing, Becker?"

I shrugged and said, "I'm still here."

"Been hearing about you. Done my heart good to see you take them whelps of Ketchum's down a peg," he said, getting down. Once on the ground, he looked critically at Chase. "Well, Gar, I see you finally got on the right side of this scrap."

Clayton was squirming in the seat, and I reckon he had been quiet just about as long as he intended to. "See here, I came out to see Miss McCray. Could you kindly tell me where she is?"

Before we could answer, Laura rushed out of the cabin and threw her arms around him. "Clayton, what are you doing here?"

It upset me some that she was so glad to see him. When I saw them together, something in me died.

Kitty and Dickie had come out on the porch and, from their expressions, I gathered they didn't care for the two dudes. Myself, I was forming a powerful dislike for the big one. I tried to tell myself that it was his surly attitude, but deep down, I knew that it was the way Laura hugged him.

I was aware that everyone except the dude and Laura was staring at me. They seemed to be expecting me to do something. Paying them no mind, I turned to go back and finish my breakfast. The sound of Laura's voice stopped me.

"Clayton, there is someone I want you to meet."

Then she introduced me to Clayton and we shook hands. His hands were as soft as a woman's, and there was no power in his grip. I could tell by his distasteful expression that he didn't care for me, and I reckon the feeling was mutual. After introductions were made all around, we went into the kitchen for coffee.

As I sipped my coffee, I felt someone staring at me. Looking over my cup, I met the cold gray eyes of Clayton Davis.

"Your West doesn't impress me much, Mr. Becker," he said. "Everyone we've met needs a few lessons in personal grooming."

I was alert enough to know that he had directed that remark at me. Maybe I did need a bath and a shave, and I suppose my clothes could use a going-over as well. But I didn't see that it was any of his concern. I dearly wanted to lean across the table and give him a taste of the back of my hand, but Laura was watching me, and so I didn't.

Then Dickie started in on me. He couldn't wait to hear about last night's events, and I recounted them to him. A time or two, I glimpsed a smile on the corner of Chase's mouth.

"Maybe I didn't hurt them much, but I gave them something to think about," I finished.

"That'll give them something to think about all right: getting even," Arky said grimly.

Now that set me to thinking. What I'd done would sure enough make them angry, and when men like that got angry, well, they just naturally did something about it.

"This matter is hardly worth discussing," Clayton announced in his stiff way.

"I intend to marry Laura and take her away from here." Then, as an afterthought, he added, "If this man Ketchum wants this land, he can have it."

Arky snorted and looked away in disgust. I'd have taken a bet that no one had ever taken anything from *him*. He might look old and harmless, but I'm here to tell you, that was one hard man. He was old because he was hard and tough. The soft ones didn't last long in this country.

"It isn't about the land anymore," Chase said quietly. His expression matched Arky's.

Dickie explained the situation with Ketchum. Arky nodded as the boy talked. "I wondered what Ketchum had against you folks," he said.

"If you leave, he should be satisfied," Malcolm said confidently.

"If the McCrays try to leave, they'll be playing right into his hand," I explained. "He'll simply stop the stage and kill them all."

"If Ketchum is wanted, why don't you have him arrested?" Clayton said, like that would settle everything.

Arky gave a harsh laugh and laid it out for them: "Where you gonna find a lawman? There ain't one in Cordell. I reckon the nearest one would be in Twin Falls." He looked to Chase for confirmation.

"That's right, and he ain't about to ride over here for a man who might be wanted in St. Louis. The only way out is to kill Ketchum." Chase nodded.

"And Barry Ferriss," I added from the window.

"Why don't some of the town's people do something about this Ketchum?" Malcolm asked. "They all seemed ready to fight *us.*"

"They ain't scared of *you,*" Arky said with a harsh laugh.

"And they *are* scared of this fellow Ketchum?" Malcolm asked with a curious expression on his face.

"Some of them," Arky explained. "Most of them have families with their own problems. They just don't want to get involved."

"Ketchum doesn't bother the folks in town," Chase said. "Most of them don't really know the McCrays, so the townfolk figure this squabble is none of their business."

"And nobody in his right mind wants to face Ferriss," Arky added grimly.

Nothing was going to come from this talk, and I was tired, so I went out to the shade of the trees, stretched out on the ground, and considered what Arky had said.

The old-timer was right. Ketchum had a rough crew and they wouldn't take my raid lying down. If Ketchum didn't let them retaliate, they would quit on the spot.

But I felt sure they wouldn't come today. No, they'd be too busy fixing saddles and rounding up their mounts. Tomorrow? That was likely. It was cool where I lay, and I drifted off to sleep.

I awoke slowly, which was unusual for me. Mostly, I awake suddenly. Groggily, I stretched and looked to the sky. The sun was high, and I judged it to be just after noontime.

As I brushed the leaves from my clothes, I saw Laura talking with Clayton on the porch. She was laughing at something he had said.

Seeing them together made me feel cold and hollow inside. Even after all the grief she had put me through, I still felt bad at the thought of her marrying Clayton.

Maybe it was for the best. I couldn't offer much to a girl like Laura. I had little money and no skills other than using a gun. Oh, I knew a sight about ranching, but I had no ranch. For the first time in my life, I realized that I had no future.

Feeling down, and meaner than a grizzly, I made up my mind to do something. If Laura wanted to marry Clayton, I'd fix it so that she could.

Chapter Eleven

I watched the Ketchum place from the same spot as the night before. What I had in mind was foolish, even crazy. I had no plan in mind. I'd just wait until my chance came, and then kill Ketchum and Ferriss.

With Ketchum out of the way, his crew would drift. All of them except Ferriss, who would hang around to have a go at me. I intended to give him his chance today.

It soon became apparent that the ranch was deserted, or nearly so. The way I had it figured, most of the hands were out hunting horses. If they would wait, most of the horses would be back by nightfall. Once they had grazed and filled their bellies, the horses would be ready to come home. Horses are a lot like humans, and like to spend nights at home. During the

139

day they may wander in search of good grazing, but come night they'll usually come back.

Judging by the movement of the shadows, I'd been waiting about an hour when both Ketchum and Ferriss came out of the big house. For a minute they stopped in the yard. They were in deep conversation and I could just guess what they were discussing.

I took off my hat, wiped the sweat from my forehead, and tried to spit. My mouth was so dry that I couldn't do it. I jammed my hat back on and dried my palms on my jeans. This was it. I was going to end things here and now.

As I stood up, Ketchum and Ferriss sauntered into the barn. Knowing that this would be my best chance, I ran down to the yard, pressed myself to the wall of the big house, and waited for them to come out.

It wasn't long before they did, but to me it seemed like forever. Stepping out in plain sight, I hollered to them and went for my gun.

It wasn't in me to bushwhack them, no

matter how low-down they were, but right then I was wishing I *had* done it.

Both men whirled, drawing as they turned. I was sure surprised at Ketchum's speed. Why, he was just as fast as Ferriss.

As I registered this, I centered my gun on Ferriss's broad chest and fired. Cocking my pistol, I put another bullet right on top of the first one.

As I turned my attention to Ketchum, something slugged me in the wind, and I went down to one knee. Out of the corner of my eye, I could see some of the hands rushing out of the bunkhouse.

Right then, I figured I had bought it, but it wasn't in me to give up without a fight. Ketchum was the one I wanted, so I paid the others no mind. I leveled my gun at him and fired. He dropped his gun and grabbed his shoulder. Before I could get off another shot, he lunged back into the dark opening of the barn.

There was an awful roaring in my head, and I could hear the sound of rifle fire all around me. Any minute now, I expected to feel the bullets tearing through me.

Lunging to my feet, I went after Ketchum. I was swaying in front of the barn when he rushed out astride a big bay. That bay banged into me and knocked me flat.

As I lay in the dirt, I knew I was in trouble. Those hands would be coming for me. Desperately, I reached for my fallen gun. But my hands wouldn't work right. They seemed unnaturally large and faraway.

It was so quiet. Was this what it was like to die? I'd always halfway expected to hear the roar and feel the heat of the fires. Maybe I'd made it to heaven after all.

Dying? The thought hit me all of a sudden, and it made me mad. I'd be hanged if I'd die before Ketchum!

With a mighty effort, I lunged to my feet, but instantly, pain knifed through my left leg. I stared at the bullet hole in my thigh. In the excitement, I hadn't even noticed getting shot there.

Swaying on my feet, I looked for someone to fight. The world spun and my eyes blurred, but through the daze I saw four men coming at me from the trees.

They appeared to be unnaturally tall as they walked slowly toward me. They had rifles, and I tried desperately to find my own gun.

It was lying in the dust by my feet. Bending over to get my gun was too much, and I caved in right there. I hit the ground with a jolt that shook my whole body. For a moment I lay there and gasped in pain. Then everything went black.

As the blackness faded I felt a blazing heat. Slowly I began to make out murmuring voices. The voices were far away, and I couldn't quite make out what they were saying.

It was too much trouble to concentrate, so I gave it up. It was so hot that my body felt on fire. Just when I thought I couldn't stand the pain any longer, something cool was placed on my head. The coolness slowly worked its way through me.

Opening my eyes, I looked around. It took several tries to get my eyes focused, but when I did, I saw I was in Dickie's room, and Garland Chase and Kitty were talking quietly off in the corner.

"Any chance of getting a drink?" I croaked.

"How do you feel?" Kitty asked, replacing the damp cloth on my forehead.

"Terrible," I answered, which was the truth. "What happened to Ketchum?"

"Dropped clean out of sight," Chase said, drawing a chair up to the bed. "Me and Arky went back and looked, but his trail vanished. We saw the rest of his crew down the road, but we didn't find Ketchum."

Now, I didn't like the sound of that. Not one bit. I knew that as long as Ketchum was alive, this thing was not over.

Kitty came back with my water, and after giving me a drink, she smoothed the blankets on my bed.

"How did I get here?" I asked, suddenly remembering those four men coming out of the trees. "Last thing I remember was four guys coming after me."

"Those guys were us. We took care of them fellers down by the bunkhouse," Chase said with a smile.

"I was kinda wondering what happened to them," I said. "Who was with you?"

"Arky, Dickie, and Malcolm."

"The little dude?" I asked, shooting my eyebrows up.

Chase nodded and chuckled dryly. "He wouldn't be left out of it. I figure he had something to prove to himself, and to someone else." He gave Kitty a sly look.

Kitty turned a little red and asked if I was hungry. After thinking about it for a minute, I decided that I was. "I'll go get you some soup," she said, sticking her tongue out at Chase.

"That little guy was white and scared plumb through, but he hung right in there," Chase told me. "You're lucky we showed up when we did. You might've handled Ketchum, but those hombres down at the bunkhouse were going to salt your hide."

"What about Ferriss?"

"Deader than a doornail. You put two bullets right through his heart."

"How's my roan doing?" I asked.

Chase gave a small laugh. "Him? He's doing better than you, I'd say. Beats all I ever did see. Most horses you couldn't keep down long enough for a wound like that to heal right, but that roan just lays there."

"He always was lazier than all get-out," I commented, thinking fondly of that horse.

"He's doing just fine, but it'll be quite a spell before you can ride him," Chase said. "Been me, I'd just have shot him."

We were quiet for a long time while I squirmed uncomfortably. I was building up to ask about Laura. When I finally did ask, I was afraid of what the answer would be. So much time had passed that anything could have happened.

"She ain't married, if that's what you mean," he said. "I figure she's waiting to hear from you."

"I don't think she wants anything from me except distance," I replied, remembering our last conversation.

"I think she would marry you." Chase got up to leave.

After he was gone, I leaned back into the pillows and tried to relax. In a few minutes Kitty came in with the soup.

"How long was I out?"

"Almost three full days," she said.

The soup was good, and after eating I felt like sleeping. It was nice and quiet, so I let go and drifted off again.

Chapter Twelve

For three more days I rested and recovered my strength. Sitting on the porch, I watched Arky and Chase trying to teach Dickie and Malcolm about ranching.

Malcolm stayed at the ranch, but Clayton chose not to. That's not to say he wasn't around, 'cause he was. He rode out from town every day.

It bothered me to see him and Laura together. He wasn't the man for her, and it was on my mind to tell her so, but I knew how she would react.

Oh, what the heck, she could do as she danged well pleased. It was clear that she was going to, anyway. Mumbling to myself, I got up and limped down to the corral. The roan managed to get up when I entered the barn. He still limped, but he tried to take a chunk out of my hide with his teeth. When he did that, I knew he was feeling better. We made a fine pair, him and me, both of us shot and limping.

Then I went out to the corral and looked over the stock. I spotted a mouse-colored horse I liked. He had well-muscled hindquarters and a wide, deep chest. This horse would be fast, a real stayer.

My saddle hung on the fence, along with my bridle and rope. Taking the rope, I dropped a loop on the horse, snubbed him up to the corral, and began to saddle up.

Kitty came out and watched me. "You seem to like ugly horses," she said, rubbing the horse's neck. I was busy tightening the cinch and didn't answer. "Go see her," Kitty urged.

I unhooked the stirrup from the saddle horn and swung up. "You take care of yourself, Kitty," I told her as I rode away.

Taking my time, I rode into town and went straight to the saloon. Four hours later, as night fell, I was still there. Right about then, things got fuzzy and I had trouble finding myself in the bar mirror. Besides that, I had built up a real good anger toward that redheaded woman.

"After all, I saved her ranch and got myself shot to boot." I wasn't even aware that I was talking out loud. "What did I get for my troubles? Nothing. Just a polite boot toward the door." I downed my drink in one single gulp. "If she was a man, I'd shoot her."

"You are most certainly right, my friend." I turned to see a little feller in a rumpled suit coming up to me. "Women, my friend, are the most infuriating creatures in the whole universe."

I looked at the blurry figure and took an instant liking to him. "Belly up to the bar, pardner, and I'll buy you a drink!" I roared, and then clapped him on the back.

"Why, that is most kind, sir. Allow me to introduce myself. I'm Jenkins—Porter Jenkins."

"Becker is my name."

"Yes, I know. I've been following your exploits of the last few days," the little dude said.

I wasn't right sure what he'd said, but it sounded mighty nice. "Hey, barkeep, pour me and my friend a drink!" I hollered, pounding my fist on the bar.

The bartender came down and poured our drinks. Being just a bit off, I didn't notice his irritation at my rowdy behavior. He was a bit put out with me, and I was soon to find out he wasn't the only one.

A huge, bearded man came up and tapped me on the shoulder. "Listen, friend, we're trying to talk business." He motioned to a table where two men sat.

"A miner," I said, taking in his muddy shirt and flat-heeled boots. "A dirty miner—that's what you are."

"Be careful, friend," the miner warned quietly.

When I'd seen the mud on his shirt, I had overlooked the size of that shirt. "I never seen a miner yet that I couldn't whip," I announced cockily.

Anger sparked in the big man's eyes, and he drew back a big scarred fist.

"Dan Becker! What do you think you're doing?"

That voice stopped the big fellow in mid-swing. "Looks like you're in real trouble now, friend," he said, laughing.

I didn't have to look to place that voice. I'd heard it and that very tone many times in the past few days.

Laura stood in the doorway with her hands on her hips. "I might have known you'd be involved in something like this!" She clenched her tiny fists.

I was mad at her, but I also felt ashamed under her scorn. Defiantly, I tried to explain: "We was just discussing each other's profession."

"Hey, friend, leave me out of it," the burly miner said hastily. I'd never figured him for a coward, but the way he threw up his hands and backed up, a person would think he was scared of Laura. "Pleased to meet you, ma'am," he mumbled, and he retreated to his table.

It seemed like the whole room was watching me all of a sudden, and it put a lot of pressure on me, because no man wants to let a woman make a fool out of him in front of other men. Some of the men in the bar were already snickering.

Feeling cornered and flustered, I tried to bluff my way out. "Who do you think you are, telling me what to do? I reckon I'm old enough to take care of myself."

That came out better than I had counted on, and I glanced around the room, expecting some support. I tell you, that saloon was filled with folks eager to do nothing but mind their own business. Not one of them looked wishful to side with me.

For a while, you could hear the dust settling on the bar, but it was just the calm before Laura's storm, and she began, "Let me tell you, Dan Becker, if you want to throw your life away drinking, fighting, and heaven knows what else, that's fine with me." Her contemptuous stare took in the whole bar. I thought maybe she was finished, but she was only getting a good breath to start in again. "And another thing, I came all the way into town just to make sure you made it okay. You should still be in bed."

Now that took the wind right out of my sails and left me befuddled. It isn't any fun to be mad at someone who is worried about your health. It also made me look bad. Here I was, chewing her out for worrying. All of a sudden, I felt like I'd been hit between the eyes with the butt end of an ax. Shaking my head to clear it, I tried to think of a reply.

I was starting to feel sorry for her when Clayton came in and took her by the arm. "I'll thank you to stay away from her," he told me. Then to her he said, "Come, let's go."

What made me boiling mad was that she went without one word of protest. It came to me that I'd come out a poor second in the whole exchange. Right then, I made up my mind to do something about it.

As I stumbled out the door, I caught sight of the couple going up the street toward the hotel. Jumping up on an empty hitch rail, I hollered at them and started to speak my piece.

Suddenly, a loud crack cut me off and I felt myself falling. For an instant, I could see bright stars in my head. Then everything went black.

Chapter Thirteen

When I came to, I was lying in a nice, soft bed. My leg, where I had been shot, hurt some, but it was nothing compared to how my head banged. It felt like someone was in there with a hammer and trying to get out.

From the looks of the room, I knew I must be in the hotel. The room was bright, so it must have been well after daybreak. I sat up in the bed, then wished I hadn't. The movement made my head hurt worse and my stomach heave. Almost wishing that someone would shoot me and put me out of my misery, I lay back and closed my eyes.

Right away, my thoughts turned to Laura, and looking back on it, I had to laugh. As was usual when she was around, I had made a fool of myself. She

155

had looked so lovely, standing there in the doorway.

Somewhere in my daydreams, the door opened and the big miner strutted in. "How're you feeling?" he asked with a knowing smile.

"Like I was kicked by a mule," I answered, trying to sit up. "You didn't hit me, did you?" I asked suspiciously. I was having trouble remembering all that had happened last night.

"No, you took a nasty fall."

His laugh was loud and booming, and it made the pounding in my head sound like a stampede. As I rubbed my head and tried to remember, I discovered a lump. It was tender, and I couldn't recall just how I got it.

"You crawled up on the hitching rail to make an announcement and it broke," the miner said between howls of laughter. "I packed you up here," he added.

"Thanks."

"Don't thank me. Your girlfriend paid for the room and had me pack you in here."

"She's not my girl," I told him. "She's got a feller."

The big man cocked his eyebrows and said, "A woman don't get that mad at a man she doesn't like," he said, shrugging. "My wife is going to bring you up some grub later."

"Thanks," I said, feeling too miserable to argue about it.

"Think nothing of it. Oh, by the way, name's Jeb Reese," he said, and he stuck out a huge pawlike hand.

"Dan Becker," I acknowledged, taking his hand.

After Jeb left, I lay back on the cool sheets. The pillow felt soft to my aching head, and I was seriously contemplating a nap when the door burst open and a big woman breezed in.

She had a florid, smiling face and was toting a tray piled high with grub. Her brown hair was piled up behind her head and held by a pair of puny-looking pins.

"Jeb said you was feeling poorly, so I brought you some food," she said, setting the tray on the bed beside me. "By the way, I'm Madge Reese, Jeb's wife. You'll be Dan Becker. We've been hearing a lot about you. It was the best thing that ever happened to this town when you run that awful Dutch Ketchum out of here." Bustling around the room, she fingered the drapes, checked the closet, and ran her finger across the top of the small dresser in the corner. "My stars! These are absolutely filthy," she said as she picked up my clothes.

I gripped tighter on the edge of the blanket and watched her carefully.

"You eat now while I go wash these," she said, tucking my clothes under her arm. "That food will put you in good health again."

When she was gone, I blew a big sigh of relief. What a whirlwind!

From that brief meeting I learned two things. Judging by the amount of food on the tray, it was easy to see why Jeb was a big man. She had brought enough food for three men my size. It was also plain to see why he was a quiet, hard-to-rile sort of man. Why, I'd be willing to bet it was months between times he got a word in on her. Still, he seemed to be real happy, and I wondered about that as I tackled the food. Well, maybe marriage wouldn't be that bad after all.

After eating my fill, I pushed away the tray, which still looked almost full. It wasn't long before my mind turned to Laura, and feeling restless, I slipped out of bed and wandered about my room.

Though my leg was stiff and sore, my side didn't bother me much, because the bullet had gone in low down on my right side. Evidently it hadn't touched anything major, and unless I moved suddenly, it gave me no trouble.

I was six feet from the bed when I heard someone at the door. Frantically, I lunged for the bed. In my panic, I clean forgot about my bum leg, and when I pushed off it gave way.

Amid my curses and a solid bang, I hit the floor. Crawling and cursing madly, I scrambled into the bed and under the covers just as Laura entered the room.

I was surprised to note that she was smiling brightly. Surprised and wary too. "Falling down again, Dan?" she asked, laughing.

Her laughter sounded bright and cheery today. It wasn't anything like the sarcastic laugh I was so used to hearing from her.

"I hear you paid for this room. I want to thank you for that."

With a laugh, she waved off my thanks, then sat on the edge of the bed beside me. "I want to thank you for everything you did for us," she said, her mood switched to serious.

Taking my hand, she looked into my face, and I could feel it turning red and hot. I was feeling flustered, as I always did when she was close. Something about her threw me off. Why, it wasn't even decent that she was in here. I wasn't dressed. Squirming uncomfortably, I hitched the blankets higher under my chin and scooted to the far side of the bed.

"I shudder to think what might've happened if you hadn't helped us," she said, edging closer.

"Well, Chase did his share," I replied uneasily. I started to run my finger around my collar when I remembered I didn't have one.

"Yes, Mr. Chase was very helpful, but without you. . . ."

"What changed your mind? Yesterday you was ready to shoot me."

"I had a long talk with Mrs. Reese last night, and another one this morning."

"You talked with her? I couldn't even squeeze a word in," I complained grumpily.

"Stop that. She's sweet and means well. Besides, she made me realize how foolish I was acting."

I began to relax and feel more comfortable. A little voice inside warned me to be careful, but I wasn't paying any heed to it.

"She also invited us over for dinner this evening." Laura looked at me hopefully.

"What will Clayton say about that?" I asked, hoping he would object. It would please me no end to smack him in the chops just once.

"Clayton left this morning. He went back to St. Louis."

"You don't seem overly upset about it," I observed.

"We had a big fight last night. He

doesn't approve of what I want to do."
She gave me a funny smile.

"Didn't you want to go back with him?" I asked, pleased Clayton was gone.

"I changed my mind. I've decided I like it here."

This was coming way too fast for me. First she wanted nothing but to get out of here. Now she wanted to stay. She liked Clayton. Then she had sent him packing. I started to ask a question, but she cut me off:

"Mrs. Reese said she would keep you from leaving town before I had a chance to speak with you. How did she manage that?"

"She stole my clothes!" I sputtered.

"It didn't hurt you any." She laughed at my discomfort. "Well, I've got some shopping to do. I need a new dress for tonight."

After she was gone, I remembered that I had never agreed to go tonight. Fact is, I hadn't gotten a chance to say very much. Was I becoming like Jeb Reese? I tried to get worked up about it, but I couldn't.

*   *   *

"Landsakes! Are you still in bed? It's almost noon," Madge Reese cried as she burst in on me.

"I couldn't very well leave as long as you had my clothes," I grumbled, knowing full well what she had in mind when she took them.

"Here they are. Nice and clean. I swear, they were absolutely filthy. You should wash them more often. A bath and a shave wouldn't hurt you, either."

Even Madge Reese has to stop for air every once in a while, and when she did, I slipped a question in on her: "What did you say to Laura? One minute she was ready to have me shot, and the next. . . ." I stopped because I wasn't real sure just what Laura had in mind. I had a sneaky suspicion, but I didn't dwell on it.

"Sonny, you have a lot to learn. All that child was telling you last night was that she cares about you very much," Madge explained.

"Well, if you ask me, that's a funny way of doing it."

Madge gave me a knowing smile that

I didn't care for. It seemed to imply something. "Well, I've got a million things to do before tonight. Are you coming? Of course you are. A new suit would be nice. They have lots of them down at the store. Maybe you should buy one." She was still talking as the door closed behind her.

I leaped out of bed and threw my clothes on as fast as I could. I was almost running when I reached the street below. Pulling to a halt, I gulped three or four mighty breaths.

"Know the feeling. Get that way myself once in a while," Jeb said, coming up behind me. "Don't worry, you'll get used to it." He clapped me on the back.

"I don't want to get used to it," I told him.

Jeb laughed heartily. "I hear you'll be coming to dinner."

"I guess so, but your wife said I need a suit and a shave."

"Women folks! They expect a man to shave every day," Jeb said in a fatherly tone.

"Every day?" I fingered my stubble and looked at Jeb's beard.

He shrugged. "A man's got to put his foot down sometimes."

Every day? Most times I went two weeks between shaves. Forgetting all about Jeb, I wandered away.

I didn't get far before I met up with the little dude from the bar last night.

"I'm Porter Jenkins. We met in the saloon last night?" He said it like a question, so I nodded impatiently. "I understand you will be in need of my services," he continued.

Again he paused, like he expected something from me. This time I didn't have a clue to what he was jabbering about.

"I'll start from the beginning," he volunteered. "I'm the only lawyer in town, and it so happens that I am also the justice of the peace." He drew himself to his full height.

"Yeah? So what?" I grunted, unimpressed.

"As there is no minister in town, I'll

have to perform the ceremony. Madge Reese mentioned tomorrow afternoon.''

Those two were planning a wedding! It was all that busybody Madge's fault. As I growled, the little guy backed up a few paces and said, "I can see you are excited about your impending good fortune. We can work out the details later."

Growling and grumbling to myself, I ambled up the street. The best thing I could do was leave town. The only reason I stayed was Ketchum. Leastways, that's what I told myself.

I'd been doing some thinking about Laura, and marriage had been in those thoughts. It seemed like everybody was pushing me into this wedding, and it was in me to rebel. Being stubborn by nature, I didn't like being pushed into anything.

The thought of leaving town brought to mind my horse. Last I'd seen of him, he was tied in front of the saloon. He wasn't there now, so someone must have led him down to the livery. Quickly, I walked down to the stable to check on him.

A square-built, powerful-looking man

was shoeing a horse out in front of the stable. I asked him if my horse was there.

"He was, but Madge Reese and that McCray girl came by this morning and took him. Everybody knows you two are fixing to get hitched, so I figured it'd be okay. Besides, they said the horse belonged to them."

Actually, the horse belonged to Ketchum, but even if he were here, he wouldn't get it back. Not after those two women laid claim to it. "You rent horses, don't you?" I asked.

"Not to you I don't. Mrs. Reese done threatened me," the hostler answered, spitting tobacco juice in the dust.

"Well, I'm threatening you too now," I said, and tried to look menacing.

"I hear tell that you're some kind of gunfighter, but I'd sooner face ten of you than Mrs. Reese." He shook his head. "Can you imagine her angry?"

I tried. One thing was for sure—her anger would be a fearful thing to behold.

"Yeah, I can." I shuddered. "And I'd just as soon not see it."

Knowing that I wasn't going to get a

horse, I went back up the street. As I passed the barber shop, I paused to think. A hot bath to soak my aching leg would be nice, and I supposed that a shave wouldn't hurt any, either.

Later on, while soaking in the tub, I thought about the predicament I had gotten myself into. Marriage? The idea had an exciting and appealing quality to it, and I let myself think about what it would be like. I had to admit that it made a pleasant picture.

By the time I'd had my shave, I was in a much better mood, and while standing on the boardwalk outside the barber shop, I contemplated about the suit.

On impulse, I went across the street to the general store. After all, I could always use a suit. The ladies in the store whispered and giggled behind my back while I picked out my suit. Hot in the face, I paid for the suit and got the heck out of there.

I decided to go put my new suit in my saddlebags. Walking down to the stable, I met a lot of folks, and all of them stared as I passed. I tried to scowl at them, but I couldn't keep the silly grin off my face.

The hostler wasn't in sight, so I walked behind the stable. Ketchum and two other men were waiting for me.

The odds were against me, but I almost welcomed them. This was the kind of activity I understood. I sure wasn't used to dealing with two conniving, underhanded women.

"Figured you boys got smart and hightailed it out of here," I said in a friendly tone.

"Not likely, Becker. We got a score to settle," Ketchum said.

"So do we," a voice called from the corner of the barn.

As if by command we all turned to look. I took the opportunity to slide the thong off my gun and drop my package.

Garland Chase stepped around the corner of the barn. "I hate to horn in," he said, "but I have some unfinished business with Dutch."

He stepped up beside me while Ketchum squirmed uncomfortably. The odds weren't what they just were, and he didn't like it.

"However, if these gentlemen want some action, I trust you will accommodate them," Chase said, motioning to the men with Ketchum.

Now, I wasn't right sure what all that meant, but if those hombres even blinked, I figured to plug them. Still, I tried to discourage them a mite. "No sense in you fellers dying," I pointed out.

"Dutch is my uncle," the young one said, his voice rising in tone with every word.

"You do what you think you have to," I agreed.

He was a good-looking youngster, and I didn't want to kill him. Too bad that boys had to grow up fast out here. As for the other one, I didn't bother talking to him. He was an older, seasoned man and would back whatever play Ketchum made.

That is the way it was for a minute, the five of us glaring at one another. Then someone moved and in unison we went for our guns.

With smooth skill, I hauled out my old six-gun and drilled the steady-looking feller twice, right through the heart. Out of the corner of my eye, I saw the kid grab his gun. He had it halfway out when he lost his grip and dropped it. Then both Chase and I had him covered.

That boy's face turned dead white, and I reckon he grew up right then and there. For a second we froze while Chase and I sort of calmed down. A shooting keys a man up tight, and it takes a second to unwind.

Glancing over, I saw Ketchum gasping on the ground. One look was all I needed to know that he was finished.

That kid swallowed hard a couple of times, never taking his wide eyes from the two guns pointed at him. "Stage'll be leaving soon, and I'd like to be on it," he suggested.

Chase nodded, and we holstered our guns. "You do that, boy," he said gently.

I picked up the youngster's gun. "You'll be needing this," I said, holding it out to him.

"You keep it. I don't ever want to see

it again," he muttered. He wiped his nose on the back of his hand.

A crowd began to gather, all of them curious to see what had happened. Jeb came loping up to examine the two fallen men. "Both deader'n a busted clock. That was good shooting, boys," he announced. "Come on, I'll set up the drinks."

I started to follow when Laura called to me. For a moment I hesitated.

"Forget him, boys. There'll be no drinking for him today," Jeb roared, slapping his thigh.

When we were alone, Laura moved up close to me. "I'm sorry to spoil your fun, Dan, but we need to talk."

"The whole town seems to think we're getting married," I said.

"I wanted you to know the marriage wasn't my idea. Madge just got carried away. If you don't want to, I won't hold you to it. Are we still going to the Reeses' for dinner?" As I nodded, she continued: "You can tell me then." She kissed me on the cheek. Then she turned around and walked away.

Chapter Fourteen

After Laura left me, I stood in silence. Recalling why I had come here, I picked up my suit and went inside the barn.

The hostler was still nowhere to be seen, so I poked around till I found my saddle. As I stuffed the suit in one of the pouches, I heard a thumping sound from the back of the barn. Slipping the thong off the butt of my gun, I cat-footed it back there.

What I found was the hostler all trussed up behind the straw. I pulled out my knife, vaulted over the straw, and cut him loose.

"Thanks, Dan. I was getting cramped back there," he said, rubbing his wrists.

"Forget it, I'm beginning to know how it feels to be tied down."

A look of pity crossed his face, and he scratched his chin. "Being tied up like that sure makes a man thirsty. Someone might steal one of my horses while I was gone for a drink," he suggested.

"I never ran from nothing in my life!" I declared loudly.

"Be smart, man. Run while you got the chance," the hostler said, almost pleading.

"You married?" I asked.

"Heck, yes. Why do you think I'm working in this stable? My wife, she wanted to settle down. Said punching cows wasn't no way to raise a family." He paused to squirt some tobacco juice in the pile of straw. "She made me buy this place and I've worked my tail off ever since."

I shook my head in sympathy, because blacksmithing was hard work. Still, I didn't think Laura would want me to get a job. I had always figured on having a nice ranch someday.

"Dan, you got that faraway look. That's the worst sign. Best thing you could do is jump on a horse right now." The hostler grabbed me by the arm. "I'm going to the saloon for a drink," he said, hitching up his pants.

Longingly, I looked to the horses in the stalls. Part of me wanted to jump on one and ride up in the hills where I could smell the pine trees and feel the wind in my face. I thought about it, but I didn't do it. The truth was, this marriage sounded better all the time. In fact, if it wasn't for this supper tonight, I'd be enjoying myself.

I'd given my word to be at that supper tonight, and I never went back on my word. Anyway, it was just supper. How bad could that be?

As night fell, I put on my suit and went over to the Reeses' house. The new suit was stiff and scratchy. The pants were slick and my gun belt didn't ride too well. In disgust, I took off the gun belt and shoved my pistol down in my pocket.

When I rapped on the door with the butt of my six-shooter, Jeb's voice boomed for me to come in. I shoved that gun back in my pocket and went inside. Jeb and Laura were seated at the table, and Madge was setting a plate the size of a small wagon on the table. That plate was piled high with slabs of meat, and I swear that table groaned a mite when she set the plate down. Then she said, "My stars, but don't you look handsome tonight, Mr. Becker. And that suit—I declare it fits you like it was made by a tailor in St. Louis."

And here I thought it was mighty tight in a few spots. Grinning sickly, I sat down at the table.

"But that collar just doesn't lay right. Here, let me fix it for you." Madge started to fuss with my collar.

I was tempted to brush her away like a fly, but instead I concentrated on my manners. I was trying to recall what my mother had taught me so long ago. It was hard, though. Been quite a spell since I had sat at a table. Of course, I'd had some practice with the McCrays lately. Recalling something Laura had said, I cleared my voice and said, "Thank you, ma'am. I'm most glad you had me over." That didn't come out real good, but I wasn't about to try again. Laura seemed pleased, so I was happy.

"It was no bother. Now let's eat. My, it has been hot lately. We need rain. 'Course, Jeb being a miner, we don't depend on the rain like the farmers and the cattlemen do. Still, my garden is absolutely drying up and blowing away."

As we ate, Madge put out a steady stream of senseless chatter. At first I tried to follow what she was saying, but it was no use.

Jeb, however, seemed to be at ease. He kept shoving food into his bushy beard, and his only contribution to the conversation was a grunt or two. I noticed that when Madge was around, Jeb became very quiet, sort of in self-defense, I reckon.

As Madge brought out the dessert, some kind of cake topped off with berries, the worst thing happened, and she started rapid-firing questions my way. "Have you thought about where you two are going to live? Do you have a job, Mr. Becker?"

My cake went down wrong, because I was having trouble swallowing around that danged tie. Spitting and sputtering,

I searched for a way out. Luckily, Laura came to my rescue.

"Dan has started building a house on our ranch. We're going to live there. Dan is going to get some more cattle, and he says some chickens and hogs too."

I choked again, and Jeb snorted. *Hogs and chickens!* Why, you couldn't tend them from the back of a horse. What was this woman trying to get me into? Boy, it was hot in here. My face sweated, and that darned suit was itching me in places I didn't care to scratch. Not right at the moment, anyway. To make matters worse, every time I moved, that danged gun gouged me.

"Tomorrow's a big day. I'd best walk you to the hotel," I told Laura, hoping we could leave.

"Yes, we should be going," she agreed, for which I was most grateful.

Being most careful of that gun, I slid out of my chair. I remembered to say thanks to Madge, and I even mentioned that all the food was mighty tasty.

"Why, for goodness sake, it wasn't any

bother," Madge said as she followed us to the door.

Looking back, I saw Jeb reaching for another piece of cake. Madge didn't look, but somehow she knew what was going on. "Jeb Reese, you stay away from that cake!" she snapped. And Jeb jerked his hand back like it had been burned.

Once outside, I stamped my feet and shook my leg trying to relieve my discomfort. I had to be mindful of the six-gun in my pocket. I didn't want it to go off.

Laura was quiet, but all the same, I knew she was waiting for an answer. All I had done was jump right out of the frying pan and straight into the fire.

"Nice night," I commented.

"Yes, real nice," Laura agreed quietly.

I could see she wasn't going to make it easy. I was beginning to see that forever is a long time.

Mopping the sweat from my face, I cleared my throat. From my pocket, I took the ring I'd bought earlier. "I know the whole town already thinks we are getting married, but I want to ask you and do it right," I said, slipping the ring on her finger.

"Oh, Dan! I'm so happy," she said, and she threw her arms around me.

You know something? Right then I wasn't regretting my decision, not one bit.

The next morning, I sat down in front of the general store and shot the breeze with all the married men in town. It seemed like everyone in the country had taken the day off. That's the way it was around here. This country was mighty shy of entertainment, and almost anything qualified.

The thought of standing up in front of all those folks made me nervous, though. By turns, I fidgeted and then the next minute I was happy and grinning like an idiot.

Garland Chase and Arky Thompson caught up with me in the hotel lobby. "We hear congratulations are in order," Chase said, holding out his hand.

I shook hands with both of them.

"Have you given any thought to how

you're going to support this wife?" Arky asked, getting right to business.

To tell the truth, I hadn't. "I figured on doing some ranching," I replied. " 'Course, I'll have to get some more cattle," I added, realizing I didn't have that much money.

Wide grins spread across both their faces, and I began to get suspicious. "That's just the very thing we came to see you about," Arky said. "Seems like there's about four hundred head of wild cows running loose."

"Yeah, they was getting real bothersome," Chase added. "You know, getting into everybody's gardens and the like. So a few of us boys rounded them up, branded them Circle B, and drove them over to the McCray place."

"Circle B, huh? Seems to me that a body could change Ketchum's Circle K into a Circle B real easy," I pointed out.

"That would be rustling," Chase said, shocked by the idea. "These cattle were running loose."

"Besides, who's gonna complain?" Arky asked.

"I don't know," I argued. "I don't like the thought of having to look over my shoulder all the time. Look what it did to Ketchum."

"Oh, it did him in all right," Chase agreed. "But he had a reason to be looking back."

"A couple of fellers came out to the ranch this morning," Arky told me. "One of them was a Pinkerton."

"That guy Ketchum killed back in St. Louis was a Pink," Chase added.

A Pinkerton! No wonder Ketchum had been worried. Those Pinkertons take care of their own.

"That Pinkerton was trying to arrest Dutch when Dutch killed him," Arky said.

"This feller this morning, he told us that there was a reward out for Dutch, dead or alive." A smile played on Chase's lips. "We told him that you was the one that killed Ketchum and that you would take the cattle as a reward."

"But you're the one who killed Ketchum," I reminded him.

Chase gave me an innocent look. "Was I? Things happened so fast."

I knew that wasn't true, but I let it pass. To tell the truth, I was glad to have the cattle.

Chase gave me a smile and a wink. "Call it a wedding present."

"When did you boys find the time to do all this?" I asked, wondering how they managed to get that many cattle branded in such a short time.

"We started while you was lollygagging around in bed," Arky explained. "We could see the writing on the wall."

"We was driving the cattle yesterday, and that's when I spotted Ketchum," Chase told me.

I'd been wondering how he'd happened to come along yesterday at just the right time.

"A big miner named Jeb Reese brought out a couple of pigs early this morning," Arky said, his tone telling me he liked pigs about as much as I did. "We penned them up for you."

"Why didn't you just shoot them?" I asked sourly.

Arky gave me a hard look. "We thought about it. It took me and Dickie an hour to build a pen. Took twice that long to get them dang pigs in it."

"I want to thank you guys for all you've done. Come out for supper sometime," I offered. "We'll be having pork chops."

At about noon, I went and had another bath and shave. It was the first time I ever did that two days in a row, but I wanted Laura to be proud of me.

Pushing through the batwing doors, I saw that the saloon was packed. That suit itched again, and I wished that I'd scratched before coming in.

"We're ready to start!" Madge cried, and she took me by the arm and dragged me up to the bar. "You stand here by Porter," she said, propping me up beside the little lawyer.

After motioning to a skinny old lady at the piano, Madge sat down. As the woman played, Laura walked in with Garland Chase. Laura was beautiful, and mine forever. I couldn't wait to get back to the ranch. When they reached us, Garland winked and stepped back.

Porter began to ramble on with the service, and my mind wandered to a mountain stream filled with fish. All of a sudden, Laura elbowed me in the ribs.

Wincing, I looked around blankly. The whole saloon was watching me, and, feeling kind of panicky, I wondered what I was supposed to do. I loved Laura, but this wedding ritual was scary.

"Do you take this woman?" Porter asked with a wave of his arm.

Beaming with pride, I said, "I do." A cheer went up from the onlookers.

From there on, the weddin' was quick and painless. After we were done, Laura told me, "Madge says it's customary for you to stand the first round of drinks, but you have just one and then come along. We need to get out to the ranch."

I saw a gleam in her eyes, and my heart raced. I pulled her close and kissed her tenderly.

The womenfolk filed out for Madge's cakes, and the bartender started pouring drinks for the men. Cost me a bundle to set them up too.

After a quick one, I hurriedly tore myself away from the party that was starting and rushed outside to my bride.

Laura was waiting in the buckboard for me. Man, she sure looked pretty. Climbing up beside her, I gathered up the reins.

"Tomorrow you can start on the house again," she said.

"And today?" I asked eagerly.

"Today is for whatever you want," she said alluringly.

You know something? I was looking forward to every minute of marriage with Laura. Me, Dan Becker, ruined for life, and loving every minute of it!